"What the hell do you think you're playing at?"

At the sudden attack, Jill spun around, clutching her towel when it threatened to fall. "I have no excuses," she said. "I knew you were going to have me thrown out so I acted on impulse to stop you."

"Which doesn't explain why you're here at all. I thought you left with Daniel hours ago."

"You musn't blame Mr. Prasad," she said hastily, afraid that he might think this was the pilot's fault. "I told him you'd invited me to stay the night."

She could hardly meet Midas's withering gaze. "Did you, now? All the same, he should have checked with me before taking your word."

"He wanted to, but I gave him the impression that you and I, that we were . . ." She couldn't go on.

"Lovers?"

Valerie Parv had a busy and successful career as a journalist and advertising copywriter before she began writing for Harlequin in 1982. She is an enthusiastic member of several Australian writers' organizations. Her many interests include her husband, her cat and the Australian environment. Valerie's love of the land is a distinguishing feature in many of her books for Harlequin. She lives in New South Wales.

Books by Valerie Parv

VALERIE PARV

That Midas Man

Harlequin Books

TORONTO • NEW YORK • LONDON
AMSTERDAM • PARIS • SYDNEY • HAMBURG
STOCKHOLM • ATHENS • TOKYO • MILAN
MADRID • WARSAW • BUDAPEST • AUCKLAND

Harlequin Presents first edition November 1992
ISBN 0-373-11510-5

Original hardcover edition published in 1990
by Mills & Boon Limited

THAT MIDAS MAN

Printed in U.S.A.

CHAPTER ONE

'HAPPY birthday to you, happy birthday to you, happy birthday, dear Mummy, happy birthday to you.'

Hearing her daughter's reedy voice, Jill Casey swallowed hard and rested her forehead against the cool glass of the telephone booth. Her knuckles whitened on the handset as she sought to control her emotions. She would get Georgina back. This was only a temporary separation. 'Thank you, Georgie, that was lovely,' she said, her voice husky with love for the child.

'Are you more than six, Mummy?'

'Yes, darling, a lot more.' Twenty whole years more, she thought with a touch of bitterness. And a lifetime away from her daughter's carefree innocence.

'Will you have a cake with candles?' Georgina demanded.

'I expect so.' It was hard for a six-year-old to imagine a birthday without a cake and candles but Jill didn't know who would provide them. Not Bill Downey, her crusty old editor at the *Sydney Voice* where she was a feature writer. And definitely not her ex-husband, Terry. He wouldn't give her the time of day, far less a birthday cake. There were few other candidates.

'I drew you a birthday card with flowers on it,' her daughter confided. 'Kay posted it for me.'

Kay Lloyd was Georgina's governess. 'Thank her for me. I'll keep the card for always,' Jill vowed. The lump in her throat was threatening to choke her. How much longer could she endure being a long-distance mother?

As long as it took to win Georgina back, answered the small voice inside her. She drew herself up to her full five feet seven inches. It wasn't much in height compared to Terry's six feet but her determination more than matched his superior physique. At present she couldn't compete with his greater material resources but she was determined to overcome this obstacle, too. If she was promoted to sub-editor—*when* she was promoted, she amended the thought—her salary would increase in line with the higher grading the job carried. Then she would have a fighting chance to appeal against the court order giving Terry custody of their daughter.

She forced herself to concentrate on Georgina's convoluted tale about some 'angry boys' who'd been bullying her at kindergarten. Suddenly, Jill couldn't keep up her end of the conversation any longer. The sound of Georgina's voice made her ache to feel the chubby little body squirming against her as she was showered with wet kisses. That was the reality. This charade of weekend visits and telephoned birthday greetings was a nightmare which she intended to end as soon as she legally could. 'Let me speak to Kay please, darling?' she said as soon as Georgina had finished her breathless account.

'I'm here, Mrs Casey.' The governess came on the line. 'I put Georgina's card in the mail to you yesterday.'

'Thanks, it was thoughtful of you.' She went on to quiz the woman about the 'angry boys' in Georgina's story and was relieved to hear that the problem had resolved itself. 'I'd hate to think the teachers allowed Georgie to be bullied,' she said.

'They assure me there's no cause for concern, Mrs Casey.'

But I *am* concerned, Jill wanted to scream at her. Couldn't she understand how helpless Jill felt, knowing that her daughter had a problem at school and there was nothing—absolutely nothing—she could do about it? Taking Georgie to the zoo and McDonald's on alternate weekends was no substitute for sharing her childish joys and fears. 'You will keep me informed?' she asked.

'Of course, Mrs Casey.' There was a note of disapproval in the governess's voice. She thinks I'm criticising her, Jill realised. About to reassure the woman, she stopped herself. She *was* critical and she had a right to be. This was an intolerable situation!

'I'll call again tomorrow,' she promised.

A sigh of resignation whispered down the line. 'Of course, Mrs Casey. Have a happy birthday.'

Have a happy birthday! The wish mocked Jill as she replaced the receiver. How could she have a happy anything until she was reunited with her daughter for good?

It was the one consequence she hadn't foreseen when she'd decided to end her marriage to Terry Casey. Not that there was much to end. Her love for Terry had died long before, killed by his womanising and his disregard for anyone's feelings but his own. The divorce had been a reprieve. Jill had never dreamed that Terry's legendary charm would fool even the family court judge into thinking that Terry was the best person to look after Georgina.

Would they have believed her if she'd told them about his affairs? Probably not. He was a silver-tongued devil, not afraid to use his position as anchorman of the country's most-watched current affairs programme to win his case. The judge thought it was the real Terry Casey. No doubt she went home to her family, thinking she'd met the man behind the image. She didn't know that there *was* no man behind the image. What you saw was what you got, off camera as well as on. Nobody knew it better than his ex-wife.

She sighed. Terry's image wasn't the reason why she'd balked at publicising his affairs at the hearing. She'd been afraid that Georgina would find out and be hurt. She was far too young to understand. Jill's own parents had divorced when she was young and she still remembered the hurt and confusion. She couldn't inflict it on Georgina.

And there was bound to be adverse publicity. Jill had kept herself and her child in the background but everything Terry did attracted attention from the media. It was a miracle that his womanising hadn't become public knowledge long before.

No, it wasn't. Jill's cornflower-blue eyes met their reflection in the glass-walled booth with wide apart frankness. His lovers hadn't betrayed him because they were as starry-eyed about him as Jill had been when they first met.

She could hardly believe that it was only seven years ago. She had been eighteen then and a cadet journalist when she was sent to interview Terry. A top-seeded tennis player, he'd been dealt a dreadful blow when a back injury had knocked him out of international competition and almost crippled him. His struggle back to fitness and his comeback attempt which ended in defeat were well documented. Jill was to report his rise, phoenix-like, from the ashes of his tennis career, to stardom as a sports commentator at the Olympics and later as a news anchorman.

An ironic smile twisted her mouth. Terry had described her story as sensitive and caring, possessing a heart. He had invited her to dinner to celebrate what he termed the first honest and accurate account of his experiences.

She should have been forewarned when he'd tried to get her into bed on their first date. Instead, she had been flattered by his attention and his charm, mistaking his lust for something deeper. It was almost a pity that she hadn't slept with him sooner. He might not have pursued her so hard, and he would certainly not have finally offered her an engagement ring, as he had when he'd realised that she would settle for nothing less.

It wasn't her intention to trap him, although he'd accused her of it later. She had truly believed—still believed, for that matter—that sex was an expression of commitment, not a—what did Terry call it?—an after-dinner minute.

She shuddered, recalling the crude expression. Had she ever been so naïve as to think it was clever?

Yes, unfortunately, she had. Her wedding photos showed how dewy-eyed she had been. When she looked into a mirror now, she was surprised that she didn't look all that much different from those photos,

if you didn't count the wariness in her gaze and a
certain tightness around her mouth.

Her eyes were still as pale blue and wide-set,
fringed by thick dark lashes. And her mouth still
turned up at the corners, making her look younger
than her years. The effect was compounded by a
dusting of honey-coloured freckles on ivory-beige
skin. It was only the innocence which was gone.

Her hair was shorter now than in her wedding
pictures. Then it cascaded to her shoulders in a silver
curtain. If anything the corona of curls which fluffed
out around her head now made her look even
younger, although inside she felt as if she'd aged
seventy years instead of seven.

At the custody hearing, her appearance had worked
against her as the judge compared her giddy blonde
looks with Terry's mature self-confidence. No wonder
she'd been found wanting.

A commotion across the road dragged her thoughts
back to the present. Lost in memories, she hadn't
noticed that there was something going on outside the
Sirius Hotel, diagonally across from where she stood.
Her journalist's instincts were alerted and she stepped
out of the phone booth to focus on the activity across
the road.

The Sirius was one of the newest and most opulent
hotels in Sydney and was already popular with celeb-
rities. The fuss was probably over the imminent
arrival of someone famous. She racked her brains but
could think of no one who warranted the gathering of
journalists, photographers and outside broadcast vans
clustered around the hotel entrance. Her editor hadn't
mentioned anything either, although he knew Jill was

coming downtown this morning. Whatever the story was, it must have broken since she left the office a couple of hours earlier.

Bill Downey would expect her to investigate and with a promotion in the air she dared not disappoint him. Still, she wished the story had happened at a more convenient time. Right now she was laden with environmental impact reports the size of telephone books, after her interview with the designers of a new expressway through Kuring-gai Chase National Park.

With a sigh, she picked up the heavy volumes and her briefcase and darted between the lanes of traffic to the Sirius Hotel. Then she saw it. Parked outside the main entrance was a gleaming red Jaguar Sovereign with the personalised numberplate, TERROR. It was Terry's media nickname and referred to his relentless style of investigative reporting. The story must be big to attract Terry's personal attention.

She hesitated. Did she really want to run into him here, in front of their colleagues? Terry could be nasty when he chose to be. He'd been dodging her calls since their divorce, asserting that anything she wanted to say to him could be relayed through his lawyer. He wouldn't welcome her presence here, even though it was pure coincidence.

Well, she had her job to do, too. If she backed away because of Terry's nastiness, and the story *was* important, it could damage her chances of promotion. And of getting Georgina back, she reminded herself. The risk of a confrontation with Terry paled by comparison.

As she approached the revolving door, a formidable

figure blocked her way. 'May I assist you with those, madam?'

The man in her path could have been a security guard or a boxer, so solid and forbidding was his stance. He could give Terry an inch in height and his broad shoulders strained an impeccably tailored suit.

Lifting her head, she gazed into a pair of cobalt eyes which emitted no light. It was like looking into the depths of an underground pool. She shivered involuntarily. 'I can manage, thank you.'

The bulky books chose that moment to begin slipping from her grasp. Instantly, the stranger pivoted to her side and lifted them from her arms as easily as if they'd been paperback novels. His dark gaze never left her face. 'It's more than my job is worth to let you struggle with these,' he said.

So he worked for the hotel. Relief coursed through her as she surrendered her remaining burden to him. He took the lot effortlessly, then gestured for her to precade him through the door.

As they were briefly confined together in the compartment of the revolving door, she was disturbingly conscious of his presence close behind her. His breath was warm on the sensitive nape of her neck. But it was his eyes which troubled her the most. She couldn't forget them, so all-knowing did they seem, as if they held the secrets of the universe in their dark depths.

What a crazy notion! He was a hotel porter, albeit an impressive one, but the Sirius was an impressive hotel and had no doubt taken care to recruit exceptional people. The secrets of the universe, indeed!

In the hotel lobby, chaos reigned. The crescent-shaped atrium which soared to a translucent domed roof was thronged with people and electronic equipment. Cables snaked across the amber marble floor and threaded the branches of the trees growing in massive pots around the atrium. Harried-looking hotel staff were trying to impose order without much success.

Zeroing in on a vacant leather armchair, she turned to the porter. He was close behind her and had his head down. Evidently, he had found something to interest him in the voluminous book on top of the pile in his arms.

'Riveting stuff, isn't it?' she said with a touch of sarcasm.

He didn't seem to notice. Without looking up from the page, he nodded. 'I've seen a few of these and always find them fascinating.'

Why would a porter be interested in environmental impact statements? Her comment had been deliberately ironic but he sounded as if he really did find the book interesting. If it was part of his training, the hotel should go into the acting business. 'You can put my things down here, thank you.' She gestured towards the chair.

'Certainly, madam.' He set the books down and placed her briefcase beside them, then stepped back.

'Just a moment.' She fumbled in her purse, wondering how much to tip him for his help. Deciding that two dollars should be enough, she took the coins out of her purse and spun around, then blinked. The man was nowhere in sight.

Oddly enough, she felt a rush of disappointment as

if a friend had left without saying goodbye. Which was ridiculous. She didn't even know his name. Perhaps the hotel discouraged tipping and he'd slipped away rather than embarrass her. Still, she felt uneasy, as if she'd missed something important.

Chiding herself for letting such a trifle bother her, she looked around the lobby. Within seconds she spotted the news editor from the *Sydney Voice*, and understood why Bill hadn't asked her to cover this story. It had been given to bigger fish. Deciding that her books would be safe enough on the chair, she collected her briefcase and approached the editor who was talking to a photographer, also from Jill's newspaper. 'What's going on, Letitia?' she asked the editor.

Letitia Ferraro flashed her a rueful grin. 'Very little as yet. John and I were hoping to meet up with Midas Thorne. He's supposed to be unveiling a radical technological advance of some kind but nobody knows what, where or when. My tip-off said it would be here, but it's beginning to look like a wild-goose chase.'

Jill wrinkled her brow. 'Midas Thorne?' Then she had it. He was the wunderkind of the engineering world, rising from humble Tasmanian birth to control of a mighty business empire which spanned the globe. She glanced around the lobby, curious to see what such a paragon looked like. 'Is he staying here?'

Letitia gave her a long-suffering look. 'My dear girl, he owns the place. He keeps two penthouse floors purely as his *pied-à-terre*.'

'How nice for him.' Jill refused to be impressed. Terry had turned her off men who had money to burn. People tended to get singed in the conflagration. 'I guess you've got this under control, then.'

'There's no need for you to hang around, if that's what's worrying you,' Letitia assured her. 'While we're cooling our heels here, the great man is probably making his announcement from a yacht in mid-Pacific, or some such.'

'If it's a public announcement, why all the subterfuge?' Jill asked, curious in spite of herself.

'I'd say we stumbled on to the story too early for Mr Thorne's liking. He prefers to pick his own time and place.'

'It sounds as if he can afford to,' Jill agreed. 'I'd better get back to the paper.'

Taking leave of her colleague, she made a slow circuit of the vast, plant-filled lobby. In spite of her anxiety about running into Terry, now that they were under the same roof she wanted to talk to him. He'd refused to see her or speak to her since the hearing. This was her golden opportunity to convince him that she needed to see Georgina much more frequently, for the little girl's sake as well as her own. Maybe she could use her birthday as extra leverage.

There he was. At the sight of her ex-husband, Jill's courage nearly deserted her until she reminded herself of what was at stake. Three months had passed since their last meeting but the sight of his athletic body and Byronic head of wavy brown hair still brought a knot of tension to her stomach. His aura of raw masculinity used to thrill her. Now it repelled her, knowing as she did how much of a tyrant he could be.

She nerved herself to approach the knot of people

around him. Recognising her, one of his assistants made way for her through the throng. Terry was firing off instructions to his secretary. Up close, his glowing tan was revealed as TV make-up. When he saw Jill, a frown made a deep V in his forehead.

'Hello, Terry,' she said softly.

'Later,' he said curtly and turned away. A ripple of dismay went around the small group.

'No, now,' she said with equal firmness. 'I need to talk to you.'

'For goodness' sake, Jill, this isn't the time. I'm about to do a stand-up for tonight's show.'

Laughter prickled through her but she recognised it as the product of nervousness and resisted it. 'There's plenty of time,' she persisted. 'Midas Thorne hasn't shown up yet.' Nor was he likely to, she thought, recalling Letitia's doubts.

Surprise coloured Terry's expression. 'Is that why you're here? I thought Ms Ferraro was covering this circus for your people.'

'She is. I'm here to see you.' She looked around. 'Is there somewhere we can talk? It won't take long.'

She could practically hear Terry weighing up his chances of getting rid of her without a scene. Then he shrugged at his assistant. 'I thought a divorce got you off the hook. But they still think they can nag you into submission.'

She saw the assistant wince. Terry had forgotten that his staff liked her. It was confirmed as they moved out of the circle, when Terry's secretary called out, 'Hey, Jill, I just remembered—happy birthday.'

'Thank you.'

Terry lifted an eyebrow. 'So I forgot. Did you come here just to remind me?'

'Hardly. As you just pointed out, I don't have a licence to remind you about anything any more.' If she ever had, she added to herself. 'I wanted to talk to you about Georgina.'

For the first time, she saw genuine concern in his eyes. 'Is anything wrong? She was fine when I left her with Kay this morning.'

'She's still fine. I telephoned her a little while ago. It's me who has the problem.' She took a deep breath. 'Terry, I can't take being a mother on alternate weekends.'

The shuttered look returned. 'You should have thought of that before you walked out on us.'

'I didn't walk out,' she said in a furious undertone. 'You drove me out.'

'The point is, you were the one to leave and the law takes a dim view of mothers who desert their children.'

'You bastard!' What had possessed her to think she could reason with him? 'I love her. I'm her mother. Doesn't it mean anything to you?'

'Of course it does.' Her hopes rose fractionally, then were dashed again when he went on. 'It means you'll be a millstone around my neck until she grows up. I'm only sorry I couldn't convince the court that seeing you at all was bad for her; then we'd be rid of you for good.'

She knew why he was doing this. Her presence reminded him of his failure as a husband. Before, he was able to brush his failures aside and go on to other things. It was the reason why he never socialised with his former colleagues on the tennis circuit. They reminded him of what he had lost. But she couldn't be discarded so readily.

Knowing the problem was Terry's didn't ease the blow to her self-esteem. She shrank back against the wall, shaken to her core. 'What did I ever do to you, except try to love you?' she whispered. 'You'd kill me if you could, wouldn't you?'

'Don't be melodramatic. I have a show to do.' He spun on his heel and returned to his crew. The circle closed around him, symbolically excluding her, and she shut her eyes against the waves of pain which engulfed her. She knew why she'd come here. It wasn't the story at all. It was the faint hope that she might be able to reason with Terry, appeal to his better nature. It was time she faced the fact that he didn't have one.

His tirade had shattered her. She felt raw and vulnerable, her throat aching with unshed tears. Her hunted gaze raked the crowded lobby. She had to get away from the prying eyes of her colleagues before she broke down and howled in front of them all.

The sign beckoned like a lifeline. 'Fire escape. No entry except in case of emergency.' Well, this was an emergency. She hurried towards the exit, fighting the tears which threatened to spill over at any moment.

Her first push made no impact on the heavy door but she put her shoulder to it, keening like a wounded animal, deep in her throat. Blessedly, the door gave and she stumbled through it. It clanged shut behind her, enveloping her in welcome silence.

The walls and floor were made of painted concrete, cold to her touch. A stark white light shone overhead, draining her skin of colour. She hardly noticed. Thankful for the sanctuary of the stairwell, she dropped on to a step and buried her face in her hands. She knew that Terry hated her but until now she hadn't suspected that he wanted to excise her from Georgina's life forever.

She had been dramatising when she'd accused him of wanting her dead, but, if there had been a clean safe way to dispose of her, he might have been tempted. As it was, he had killed her in his mind. How long would it be before he turned Georgina against her, too?

Happy birthday, she thought bitterly. Misery overwhelmed her and her shoulders shook as she succumbed to it. Some birthday! Her gifts were alienation from the child she loved more than life itself, and vilification by a man who'd hurt her far more than she had ever done him. 'What am I going to do?' she cried aloud.

'You could start by telling me about it,' came a resonant voice close to her ear.

Her heart leapt with fright and she jerked back to look into a pair of diamond-bright blue eyes. 'You!' she gasped, her voice hoarse from crying.

'You make me sound like the last person you want to see right now,' he said gravely, then smiled. It was as if a spotlight had been turned on in the stark stairwell. Warmth washed over her and she found herself automatically leaning towards its source. She gathered herself together with an effort. 'I know I shouldn't be here but I needed to be alone for a few minutes.'

He nodded in understanding. 'I wasn't going to

chase you away. Take all the time you need to compose yourself.'

'Thanks.' She dabbed at her eyes with a handkerchief and forced a smile. The man's dynamic presence had somehow alleviated her need to cry. 'Whatever they teach you at hotel school, it works. You have a marvellous bedside manner.' She coloured, realising how her words could be taken. 'I didn't mean. . .'

He laughed, a warm caramel sound which made her wish he would do it again. 'I know exactly what you meant and thank you for the compliment. But I misled you. I don't work here.'

The hairs lifted slightly on the back of her neck. 'Then who *are* you?'

He offered his hand. 'A fellow refugee.' The dark eyes were suddenly alive with merriment.

'A fellow. . .oh.' Understanding came swiftly. 'Don't tell me *you're* Midas Thorne?'

'Very well, I won't tell you.'

'But you are, aren't you?'

He inclined his leonine head. 'Guilty as charged. Disguising myself as your porter was an efficient means of evading the howling mob outside.'

He evidently didn't realise that she belonged to that self-same mob. 'Very clever,' she dissembled. 'No one would look twice at a porter.'

'You didn't, did you?'

She grimaced. 'I was suspicious,' she said in her own defence. 'You don't look like the average porter. Your eyes. . .' Her voice tailed off. She wasn't sure she wanted him to know how strongly he'd affected her already. 'You don't look like a porter,' she finished lamely.

'I'm delighted to hear it.' He dropped down beside her, heedless of any damage he might do to his designer suit. 'Now you know my name, how about telling me yours? I already know what kind of work you do.'

'You do?'

'The environmental impact statements. Let me guess. You're a secretary to an environmental engineer.' He frowned and butted the palm of his hand against his forehead. 'I shouldn't jump to conclusions, should I? You're probably the environmental engineer yourself.'

'No, I'm not.' She was glad that she could be at least partially honest with him. She had a feeling that he wouldn't welcome the news that she belonged to the group he was evading. 'I'm Jill Casey.' She offered her hand.

He shook it solemnly and heat travelled along her arm from his touch. 'All the same, Jill Casey, it was an unfair assumption. You can call me a male chauvinist pig if you like.'

Laughter rippled through her. 'I hardly think your lapse deserve such a harsh label.'

'You're very forgiving, ma'am. Being a refugee is turning out better than I expected.'

For her, too, she realised, aware that her impulse to burst into tears had vanished completely. She was too intrigued to be miserable. Midas Thorne's positive attitude was infectious, probably partly explaining his business success. 'You shouldn't have to go through this,' she said, indignant on his behalf. 'Isn't there a back way you can use?'

'Not tiring of my company already?' He dismissed

her denial with a grin. 'Your concern is refreshing. But my private elevator is being serviced and this *is* the back way. There's a staff entrance but the vultures are watching that as well. So here I am for the moment.'

'I see.' She wrapped her arms around her knees and rested her chin on them, then chuckled softly.

He eyed her curiously. 'What's so funny.'

'I was thinking how close I came to giving you a two-dollar tip.' Her head tilted to one side. 'Is your name really Midas?'

'Actually it's Michael. Midas was coined during the nickel boom when my business really started to take off. It stuck. These days, only my mother remembers that I have another name.'

It must be the unusual setting which had prompted her to ask such a question. 'I'm sorry, it's none of my business,' she apologised belatedly.

He frowned. 'Don't spoil a promising start. I'm enjoying being treated as a normal human being. Or are you this caring with everyone you meet?'

She glanced away, remembering why she had sought refuge in the stairwell. 'Sometimes I wish I didn't care so much,' she confessed.

'Ah, the tears.' He folded his arms across his broad chest. 'Want to talk about it?'

Oddly enough, she did, to him. He might think she was a caring person but it took one to know one. Tycoon he might be, but he was also kind and considerate. It showed. 'It's a long story,' she warned him.

'We could be here for a while.'

Haltingly at first, then more freely, she told him

about her marriage break-up and the heartache she'd
endured when her ex-husband had gained custody of
Georgina. 'I just couldn't compete. He can give her
so much more than I can, a full-time governess, better
schools, overseas travel.'

'But not a mother's love,' Midas intervened.

'Not even a father's love,' she said bitterly. 'I'm
sure the only reason Terry wanted Georgina was to
punish me for leaving him.'

'He doesn't like children?'

'Oh, he loves her in his own way. But what will
happen when he has to choose between her and his
own pleasures?'

'As in other women?' She nodded glumly. 'I see.
But surely the court took that into account.'

Again she shook her head. 'I couldn't tell them the
extent of it. My parents divorced when I was young
and I've never forgotten how they tore each other
apart, hurling accusations and counter-accusations at
each other. I never knew what was true and what was
said to wound. It's not fair to divide a child's loyalties
the way mine were. I couldn't do it to Georgina.'

'Not even to have your daughter back?'

'Not even for that.'

He touched a finger under her chin, lifting it
slightly so their eyes met. 'I was right about you. You
do care about people. But you should care for yourself, too. You're supposed to love your neighbour *as*
yourself, not more than or instead of.'

'I'll try to remember.'

Above their heads, a door opened on the landing of
the next floor. Jill's head jerked back in alarm but
Midas rested a reassuring hand on her wrist. 'It's all

right, he's one of my people.' He stood up and
brushed the dust off his trousers. 'What's the news,
Ted?'

The man leaned over the railing. 'They've got your
private elevator going again. It's waiting for you on
the next floor.'

He helped Jill to her feet. 'It looks as if the party's
over.'

She gave him a shy smile. 'It was nice meeting you.
Goodbye, Midas Thorne.'

His warm gaze stroked her face, feature by feature,
as if he was committing it to memory. 'It doesn't have
to be goodbye. Why don't we continue this discussion
in my suite?'

CHAPTER TWO

WHAT would have happened if she'd accepted Midas Thorne's invitation to visit his penthouse suite? The question bothered Jill as she tried to concentrate on writing her article about the new road through Kuring-gai Chase. But the very sight of the bulky environmental impact statements cluttering her desk reminded her of her meeting with Midas Thorne.

If he'd known she was a journalist, would he have been so considerate? From his attitude towards her colleagues in the hotel lobby, she doubted it. Describing them as a howling mob and as vultures didn't make it sound as if he held the media in high esteem.

All the same, his offer had been tempting and she had a feeling he'd known she wanted to come. Midas Thorne intrigued her as few other men had ever done. But he was rich and powerful and, as such, he scared her. Look what Terry's wealth and power had done to her. Did she want to risk a repeat performance?

She told herself she was reading too much into a simple invitation. He probably felt sorry for her, that was all. How many women did he run across sobbing their eyes out on a fire-escape? It must have been a novel experience for him. The rich were supposed to crave novelty, weren't they?

Putting the experience into this perspective helped to some extent. At least it enabled her to finish writing the environmental story, although it was only minutes short of her deadline.

'Do you get a kick out of elevating my blood-pressure?' Bill Downey asked when she dropped her copy on to his desk.

She regarded the editor blankly. 'What do you mean?'

'Making me guess whether your copy's going to be on time. Or is it a new kind of stress test?'

'Very funny.' All the same, she felt a twinge of alarm. If Bill wasn't happy with her performance, would he still recommend her for promotion at the end of the month when the present sub-editor left to have her baby?

'You're forgiven,' he said, relieving her mind. 'But only because your copy never needs much blue-pencilling. So stop looking so devastated. You make me feel like a monster.'

Her spirits lifted. 'Under that hard exterior——'

'Beats an even harder heart,' he growled before she could finish. 'Get out of here, and take this with you. It's your next assignment.'

She accepted the folder he held out. 'What's the story?'

'Given up reading, have you?'

She gave a mock salute. 'No, Bill. I'll read the file.'

'It's a tough one,' he warned as she moved away. 'But the publisher has his heart set on it, so don't disappoint him, will you?'

Her sense of unease returned. 'Any reason why this story is so important to him?'

'Not to him. To you. He's getting ready to make a decision about Helen's replacement.'

The editor's message was clear. How she performed on this story would influence whether or not she got the sub-editor's job. She hugged the folder. 'I'll do wonders with it,' she promised.

'You can try but, as I told Mr Savareid this morning, he's wishing for the moon.'

Gordon Savareid was the publisher of the *Sydney Voice*. The story must be a tough one if Bill doubted her ability to pull it off. All the more reason to prove him wrong, she thought as she waltzed back to her desk.

Moments later, she was starting to think that Bill was right. She couldn't produce the celebrity profile Mr Savareid wanted, especially after reading the background material in the file. The person she was supposed to interview in depth was, of all people, Michael 'Midas' Thorne. The file made it abundantly clear why he would never agree, and why he hated all journalists with such passion. He blamed all of them for the death of his wife and baby son.

His hostility towards the media was understandable. Six years ago Midas, his wife, Yolande, and their son, Michael Junior, had been holidaying at Byron Bay on the north coast of New South Wales. Yolande had been suffering from postnatal depression, a severe bout according to Jill's file. Somehow, the Press had discovered their hideaway. Although Midas had begged them to leave his wife alone, the journalists had chronicled her every move, snapping unflattering pictures of her on the beach, at the house, and even breast-feeding the baby. Desperate to escape the attention, she had climbed into her car, strapped the baby into the seat beside her, and driven off.

There were several places where the road went almost to the cliff edge and at one of these places Yolande had lost control of the car, plunging it into the sea. Officially it was an accident but Midas held the Press responsible. If they hadn't hounded his wife so, she wouldn't have felt the need to escape and his family would still be alive.

By the time she closed the folder, Jill's eyes were moist. That poor man! He had comforted her over the loss of her child, but she still had the hope of a reunion. For Midas, there was no such hope.

Sadness bowed her shoulders as she made her way back to Bill's office. As if it was fragile china, she placed the file on his desk. 'You're right, I can't do it,' she said flatly. 'That poor man deserves his privacy after all we've put him through.'

Bill's eyebrows arched. 'We? It wasn't the *Voice* which harassed his wife to death.'

'It makes no difference. He won't have anything to do with the media and I can't say I blame him.'

Bill looked thunderous. 'Wait a minute. Whose side are you on?'

'Justice, I hope. Why do we need this story, anyway?'

'For the very reason you don't want to tackle it. No writer has been able to get close to Midas Thorne. He's on the verge of a big business announcement. A personal profile on him, run at the same time as the announcement, would send our circulation through the roof.'

Her eyes narrowed. 'You said yourself it was wishing for the moon.'

The editor shrugged. 'There's another saying, "Seek and ye shall find".'

'What if I don't find?'

'Mr Savareid will tell me to give the story to Jeff Pullen.'

A weight settled on her chest. 'Is Jeff the other candidate for the promotion?'

'I'm afraid so.'

'But Jeff is. . .' She didn't need to finish the thought. They both knew that Jeff Pullen was totally unprincipled. He used any and all methods to get his stories, including going through people's dustbins to reveal more about them. While nobody liked his methods, he had a strong readership. Jill could hardly bear the thought of Jeff going after Midas Thorne. If Midas thought he'd met the dregs of journalism now, just wait until he fell victim to the likes of Jeff. 'You can't give him the story,' she stated.

'Then you'll do it?'

'I'll try.' Even if she didn't get an interview, she could warn Midas about the alternative. If he would speak to her at all, she thought with a sinking heart. She had been so sure that the sub-editor's job was within her grasp. Without it she had little chance of fighting for Georgina's return, yet both goals now seemed unattainable. Dismally, she picked up the file again. 'How long have I got?'

'As long as it takes. Given Mr Savareid's personal interest in this story, I'm putting you off all your other assignments. I shan't expect you back in the office until this is written.'

In other circumstances the assignment would be a dream, she realised as she cleared her desk. An open deadline, no other stories competing for her attention, and the publisher himself awaiting the results. But even if her heart had been in the story, this was mission impossible. Her sympathy was with Midas. He was entitled to some peace and privacy.

By the time she reached her Balmain flat, she knew what she was going to do. She would contact Midas, confess that she was a journalist, and explain her predicament. He had been so understanding about Georgina yesterday; he might agree to supply her with some kind of story, to keep the *Voice* from bothering him further.

Just when she managed to convince herself that pigs could fly, the doorbell rang. On her doorstep stood a courier in the uniform of a well-known florist. His arms were filled with flowers. 'There must be three dozen roses here,' she said in astonishment. Had someone remembered her birthday after all?

'Six,' the courier amended.

When he'd delivered them and left, she stood staring at the flowers in amazement. The roses were a glorious golden colour, as radiant as morning sunshine. With trembling fingers, she reached for the card nestled among the fragrant blooms.

'To Jill Casey—remember the golden rule.' The card was signed 'Midas Thorne'.

He couldn't know it was her birthday, so the flowers were meant to cheer her up, she realised. How had he learned her address? She dismissed the question almost at once. Men like him had far wider resources than most people. He probably had a battery of assistants taking care of details like this. Still, the gesture made her feel cherished and special.

Her senses swam as the perfume pervaded her small flat.

Or was it the hand-written card which had brought Midas Thorne close? The writing was strong and masculine. It could be his own. She pulled her hand back, aware that she was crushing the card against her breast.

An image of him, tall and virile, dominating the stark stairwell, rose up before her. Her muscles weakened as she recalled the radiance of his smile. His thoughtfulness made her want to cry, and she buried her face in the massed blooms, drawing their fragrance into her lungs as if it was the breath of life itself.

It was so long since anyone had cared about her that she was in danger of confusing his thoughtfulness for something more personal. It was tempting to believe that he had sent the flowers because he had been as intrigued by her as she was by him. A shudder shook her and she became aware of a deeper, more intimate yearning. Lifting her head, she met her reflection in the mirrored wall, her expression appalled. Her imagination had made her a writer, but she mustn't let it run away with her.

She must face facts. The flowers had been dispatched by some secretary, no doubt at Midas's bidding, but the handwriting she was mooning over so foolishly probably belonged to the florist, or an uninterested member of Midas's staff.

There was one way to prove it to herself and that was to contact him. If, as she anticipated, he was unavailable, she would know exactly where she stood.

Nevertheless, it was next morning before she summoned the courage to telephone him, after looking up his company in the telephone book. She told herself she needed the previous evening to study the file she'd brought home with her. Besides, she didn't have a private telephone number where she could reach him outside business hours.

Excuses, excuses, she told herself as she dialled his office number. The truth was, however much she expected his rejection, she was postponing it as long as she could.

'I'll put you through to Mr Thorne's private secretary,' the switchboard operator informed her.

Music hummed on the line briefly, then a crisp voice announced, 'Mr Thorne's office. Sarah Brent speaking.'

Even as she gave her name and asked to speak to Midas Thorne, Jill wondered why she hadn't said she was from the *Sydney Voice*. Was it because she knew he would refuse to take her call? And she wanted very much to speak to him again, in spite of her arguments to herself.

Tension radiated down her arm and she forcibly relaxed her grip on the receiver. 'I'm sorry to keep you waiting. Mr Thorne is in a meeting,' his secretary said.

Her spirits plummeted, even though she had steeled herself to expect this. 'I understand. Will you tell him that Jill Casey called to thank him for——'

'Just a moment, Ms Casey. He's just walked in.'

So he hadn't been evading her after all. Jill resisted the pleasure which spiralled through her at the thought.

The eddies of delight intensified when she heard his voice. 'Well, good morning, Jill Casey. Feeling any better today?'

'Wonderful, thanks to your surprise. Yellow roses are my favourites.' Now why had she told him that? Unless it was to soften the blow of what she had to say next.

His throaty chuckle sent goose-bumps sizzling down her spine. 'The florist is the psychic one, not me. When I described you to him, he insisted that yellow roses would be your flower.'

So he *had* chosen the blooms himself. Surprise and wonder made her a little light-headed. Suddenly she knew she couldn't tell him about her job and spoil the moment. Better just to ring off quickly. 'All the same, I wanted to thank you. I'm sorry if I interrupted a meeting.'

He sensed that she was about to hang up. 'It's all right, my meeting is over. Don't you want to know how I tracked you down?'

'I admit, I was curious.'

'I memorised the luggage tag on your briefcase when I carried it into the hotel for you,' he said with an edge of triumph in his voice. He was obviously proud of his memory. The small vanity made him seem more vulnerable, somehow.

'I'm impressed,' she said, laughter in her voice. 'I was giving all the credit to your staff.'

There was a slight pause during which she could hear his breathing deepen. The intimate sound made her pulses quicken. 'I expect you to make amends for failing to appreciate my talents.'

A delicious sensation that was half fear and half

hope made her catch her breath. 'What did you have in mind?'

'Lunch today. I have another meeting in a few minutes but it should be over by noon. I'll send a car to bring you to my office.'

He took it for granted that her answer was yes, she realised a little breathlessly. Now was the time to tell him about herself, while he could still change his mind about seeing her again. She took a deep breath. 'There's something you should know first.'

'Tell me at lunch,' he forestalled her. 'A free-for-all is about to erupt in the boardroom unless I step in and referee. Here's Sarah to set up the lunch details.'

Then he was gone and his secretary was arranging to have her brought to Midas's office. Hanging up the phone, Jill stared at it in a daze. She still hadn't told him she was a journalist and now she was seeing him socially. It would be much harder to break the news to him across a luncheon table set for two.

The thought of seeing him in a more intimate setting made her feel hot and flustered. It was what she wanted, she acknowledged, but he was going to wonder why she hadn't mentioned her job before accepting his invitation. Worse, she had allowed him to think she was something she wasn't. Or at least she hadn't corrected his impression that she was a secretary in the environmental field. She debated whether to call him back. Her hand was on the receiver when she remembered that he'd be in the boardroom by now. She didn't want him to get the message second hand. It would be better to tell him herself as soon as she got there. He would probably send her away but it was her own fault. She shouldn't have allowed the misunderstanding to continue this long.

Since she only intended to explain what she did for a living, what she wore hardly mattered. All the same, she found herself taking an inordinate amount of care over her clothes and make-up.

After trying on and discarding several outfits, she wore a knitted cotton vest and matching double-breasted cardigan. The set was banded in khaki, navy and white, over navy culottes. The outfit was dressy enough for most luncheon venues but wouldn't look out of place in an executive dining room if that was where Midas entertained her. *If* he entertained her. The invitation would probably be withdrawn once he knew more about her.

Trying to convince herself that it didn't matter either way, she brushed her hair into a shining corona, held in place by tortoiseshell combs at each side. She had never wanted for male company, turning down as many invitations, usually from colleagues, as she accepted. Her looks helped, she admitted it, although, as she applied her make-up, she wished she looked a little more sophisticated. Maybe men liked women who looked as young as she did.

So she wasn't flattered by Midas Thorne's apparent interest in her. She was intrigued by the man himself. Self-made, he wielded enormous influence in the business world and, although reputedly fair, was considered ruthless by those on the receiving end of his corporate raids. His recent forays were docu-mented in the files she'd brought home. But there was very little about him as a person. Who *was* Midas

Thorne? Bill Downey was right. It would make a sensational story.

She couldn't really justify her interest as professional. The truth was she wanted to know more about him to satisfy her own curiosity, which had been growing since those few moments on the stairwell.

This time, her arrival at the Sirius Hotel was much more streamlined. A Mercedes limousine whisked her from her flat to the hotel and an aide escorted her to Midas's private elevator which deposited her on the higher floors of the building which served as Midas's corporate headquarters. His penthouse occupied the topmost two floors of the building.

By the time she reached his suite of offices, Jill was awed by what she had seen. Terry's lifestyle had seemed luxurious but it paled beside Midas Thorne's. He obviously worked hard and his achievements were all the more impressive for knowing that he'd started with nothing. But he also lived in a style beyond Jill's previous imaginings. She wondered what his penthouse looked like, if the opulence around her was his workplace.

'The view is glorious, isn't it?' his secretary commented, hearing Jill's indrawn breath as she was shown into Midas's office.

Beyond an enormous chrome and black leather desk, the whole of Sydney was spread out at her feet, visible through a wall of tinted glass. This must be how an eagle felt, hovering over the world of men.

She looked around. 'Where is Mr Thorne?'

'He sends his apologies. The meeting shouldn't last much longer and the helicopter is standing by.'

Her confusion increased. 'Helicopter?'

'To take you to Vincero. Can I get you anything while you wait?'

Dumbly, Jill shook her head. She needed some time to assimilate the secretary's words, and she was thankful when Sarah Brent returned to her own office. Vincero was Midas Thorne's island in the Hawkesbury River, north of Sydney. When he'd asked her to lunch, she had never dreamed it would be at his secluded retreat. An item from the file screamed through her mind. 'To Midas Thorne, Vincero is hallowed ground. No journalist has ever set foot on the island and its owner has made it clear that they would not be welcome.'

That Midas wanted to take her there suggested a more than passing interest in her. She couldn't bear the thought of disappointing him now. She shouldn't have come in the first place.

Intending to call him later, she stood up and reached for her handbag, half wishing that she *were* a bird who could fly from this eyrie as effortlessly as a winged creature. She felt like a total fraud, dreading Midas's response when he knew the truth.

'Hello, Jill. I trust you've been well looked after?'

At the first sight of him, her resolve began to ebb. His sheer physical magnetism held her in thrall and she watched him place some papers on his desk with the same intensity with which a starving person watched food being served.

His fluid movements hinted at a powerful musculature. The strong lines of his face were softened by a wide generous mouth, etched with character lines.

Those devastating eyes searched her face, as penetrating as a laser light illuminating an invisible signature. She felt as if she was falling into an abyss—and enjoying it.

She could hardly breathe for the tension gripping her. If only she *had* been the secretary he'd mistaken her for, how much simpler everything would be. Her secret made a painful lump in the middle of her chest and she pressed a closed fist to it, knowing that only the truth could relieve it. 'I can't keep our lunch date,' she said, determined to get it over with. 'There's something you don't know about me.'

'You're still married?'

'No, I'm divorced as I told you.'

'Then what?'

She dragged air into her lungs, searching for the right words. Before she could find them, Sarah Brent's voice came over the intercom. With a frown of annoyance, Midas flicked it on. 'Yes, Sarah, what is it?' His voice betrayed his irritation.

The secretary explained that a complication had arisen out of this morning's meeting. Midas listened for a few minutes then thumbed the intercom off. 'I'll have to straighten this out before we leave. Do you mind waiting a little longer?'

'I shouldn't stay at all. You're busy and. . .'

His eyes darkened. 'It must be some confession if you've decided to run away. I can't have that.' He returned to the intercom. 'Sarah, tell Daniel to take my guest to Vincero and look after her until I get there.'

He meant to send her to his special island without giving her the chance to explain why he wouldn't want her there at all. A tiny spark of elation flared inside her. She should insist on telling him but, if he didn't want to hear, she wasn't responsible. Perhaps when they were at his home he would treat her revelation more fairly. His tragedy wasn't her fault. Blaming her was as illogical as holding all doctors responsible for the loss of one patient.

He waited until she nodded acceptance of his suggestion, then picked up some files and left.

Moments later, another man entered so quietly that he was beside Jill before she realised anyone had come in. She started as the stranger loomed over her. Then his face creased into a smile. 'I'm Daniel Prasad, Mr Thorne's personal pilot. Are you ready to leave?'

Quieting her leaping nerves, she stood up. 'I guess so.'

'Then I'll show you the way to the rooftop helipad.'

Murmuring her thanks, she followed the pilot to yet another elevator which served the corporate complex only. While they waited for the lift, she studied the pilot. His *cafe au lait* skin suggested an Indian heritage, although he spoke with only a faint accent. His hair and eyes were blue-black and his smart uniform skimmed an athletic body.

'Have you been with Mr Thorne for long?' she asked to fill the silence.

'A year, ma'am, since I came to Australia from Fiji.'

He was also appraising her surreptitiously, she realised gradually. Her mind burned with questions. Did Midas have many female luncheon guests, or was it a rare occurrence? While suspecting it was probably the latter, she wished it was the former. If she was special, as Midas had suggested, she had no right to postpone her confession. She could have blurted out the truth. It would have taken only a second, then she could have fled and he wouldn't have stopped her. The real reason for her silence weighed upon her. She didn't want to leave. The eventual let-down would be much harder but she seemed unable to prevent it.

The helicopter sat atop the building like a giant bird. In cream streaked with red and blue markings, it seemed to strain at its moorings. 'It's beautiful,' she breathed, admiring the sleek lines.

Daniel Prasad patted the craft as if it was a thoroughbred. 'It's an Agusta 109, a dream to fly.'

It was certainly a dream to ride in, she thought as he opened the wide side door and helped her into one of the aircraft-styled seats upholstered in plush red fabric. Two sets of seats faced each other and she took a forward-facing one, buckling herself in as her heart picked up speed. Daniel jumped into the pilot's cabin and began take-off procedures.

Soon the craft began to buck as the rotors made their first lazy circuits in the air. She braced herself for take-off. Abruptly, the passenger door was flung open. 'I made it after all. Now I can share your first impressions of my home.'

Midas hurled himself into the seat beside her and snapped his seatbelt fast. The door swung closed and Daniel resumed his pre-flight checks.

Then they were airborne. Although it was her first ride by helicopter and her senses were immediately assaulted by a myriad clamouring impressions, she was fully conscious of only one: the heady awareness that Midas Thorne was at her side, their bodies lightly touching as they swayed in harmony with the chopper's banking turn. His body heat surged through her linen culottes, infusing her with answering warmth. She had no right to be here, yet she couldn't rid herself of the absurd conviction that she was going home.

CHAPTER THREE

VINERO was located close to Kangaroo Point over-looking Brooklyn Waters and the placid expanse of the Hawkesbury River to the north of Sydney. The luxurious cabin of the helicopter reminded Jill of a jet airliner and the beat of the rotors hardly reached her ears. Far too quickly, the northern beaches dropped away and the Hawkesbury wound beneath them, criss-crossed by the sentinels of oyster beds around the township of Brooklyn.

'Is Vincero accessible by road?' she asked.

He shook his head. 'I vetoed a bridge to the mainland. You have a choice of fast launch or this.'

He gestured around the cabin and her eyes sparkled, reflecting her excitement. Arriving by boat could hardly compare with swooping out of the sky in a high-performance twin-engined executive helicopter.

Midas pointed suddenly. 'There's Vincero.' They were approaching an almond-shaped island, its sides cloaked in green. They were almost upon it when Jill glimpsed the house, an imposing Georgian mansion set high above the floodline, facing due north amid the towering gums. The views must be magnificent!

With the grace and lightness of a dancer, they set down on a grassy pad close to the water's edge. The lawns extended all the way from the house to a private jetty below them, and a pebbled walk led up to the house. Behind it rose a steep escarpment clothed in rain-forest.

'What a marvellous place,' she said, hardly aware of having voiced the thought.

'It is, isn't it? Welcome to Vincero.'

'I shall win,' she said in the same wondering tone.

'You recognise the name?'

Her eyes shone. 'Puccini's aria, "Nessun Dorma" from *Turandot*,' she said. 'It fits this place so well.' And Midas Thorne, she added silently. Winning would be second nature to him, she guessed.

'The first time I saw the island, I could imagine the tenor singing the Vincero part,' he went on.

The soaring notes of the aria filled her thoughts as she looked around. Everything about the island possessed an uplifting beauty, from the rain-forest-clad hills to the river encircling the island like an emerald necklace. In front of the house, a free-form swimming pool was carved out of the sandstone bedrock, with a waterfall spilling into it at one end. At the other, a pebbled beach gave the pool a totally natural appearance. There were several buildings clustered around the main house, she noticed. Were they guest accommodation or offices? 'I'd love a tour of the place,' she said.

His laughter showed that he approved of her enthusiasm. 'It will be my pleasure, after we've had some refreshment.'

On a terrace in front of the house, a table was set with a bottle of Mouton-Rothschild champagne in a silver bucket, paper-thin crystal glasses and a tray of hors d'oeuvres. The pilot must have radioed ahead, alerting the staff to have everything ready the moment they set foot on the island.

Midas poured some pale gold-coloured liquid into a glass and handed it to her, then raised his own glass. 'To beauty.' His dark-eyed gaze lingered on her, emphasising his meaning.

A ripple of awareness surged up her spine and she basked in the glow of his appreciation. It had been a long time since she'd been made to feel so desirable. And Midas managed it effortlessly, just by a word or gesture. How would it feel to be the object of his desire?

About to touch her glass to her lips, she hesitated. She had no right to think such things, knowing she was here under false pretences. She set her glass down.

His eyebrows arched questiongly. 'You aren't drinking?'

'There's something you must know before we go any further. I've already put off telling you for too long as it is.'

'Go ahead then. I'm listening.'

He made it sound so easy. 'I'm. . . I'm not what you think I am,' she said. 'I'm not an environmental secretary, or any kind of secretary for that matter.'

His expression became serious. 'Then what?'

This was more difficult than she'd imagined. 'I'm. . . I write for a newspaper,' she finally managed.

The disgust which distorted his noble mouth was almost more than she could cope with. 'You're a journalist?'

She had to do something, anything, to stop him

looking at her as if she'd just crawled out from under a rock. 'I tried to tell you but you wouldn't let me.'

'What about the environmental impact statements?'

'They were background for a story. Oh, please, Midas, don't look at me like that. It wasn't my fault that you jumped to the wrong conclusion.'

His eyes were inky pools of murderous fury. 'You didn't try very hard to correct my assumption.'

Her hands fluttered in the air. 'For the very reason that I knew you'd react as you're doing now.'

Most of the colour drained from his face. 'If you know that, then you must know why as well.'

It was too late to pretend ignorance. 'I read the story in the newspaper files.'

'So you *are* here on assignment?'

'Not entirely!' The cry was wrung from her. 'When we first met I didn't know who you were, I swear. Then when you were so nice to me on the stairs, I found I wanted to know you better. The assignment came much later. I didn't want any part of it.'

'Yet you're here. Do you deny that it's at your paper's bidding?'

She would have given much for the right to deny it, but she couldn't. 'I'm up for promotion. If I don't get it, I have next to no chance of fighting for custody of my daughter. My editor made it clear that the promotion depends on how I handle this story.'

Midas's lip curled. '"This story" meaning me, I gather?' He made a slashing movement with his bladed hand. 'You make me sound like a commodity you can trade for favours from your editor.'

Distress made her shake from head to foot. 'You're

painting me as some kind of vulture. I'm not, honestly.'

'Hardly a word I expect from you,' he suggested coldly. 'I gather that the daughter business was a play for my sympathy so I'd agree to give you a story. Do you have a child, or is she a convenient fiction?'

Something snapped inside her. 'Hardly, when it's obvious that you don't have a shred of sympathy in you. You, of all people, should understand the devastation of losing your child, the sleepless nights and lonely days when you ache to hold her in your arms, knowing it isn't possible. But don't trouble yourself, I'll find another way. Somehow, some way, I'll get Georgina back. Is that real enough for you?'

Choked with emotion, she swung around towards the helicopter, hardly aware of where her feet were taking her. She only knew she had to get away from this fiend who was every bit as bad as Terry, urbane and charming on the outside, but with a heart of solid granite.

'Jill, wait.'

Her glazed eyes met his blue ones as she looked back, her face a mask of misery. 'What?'

His bleak expression tore at her. He *did* know how she felt about Georgina. It was there in his agonised expression. 'I'm sorry for what I said about your child,' he said with difficulty. 'But you must understand how I feel, too. There's no way I can let you stay now.' The resonant tone shattered into a hoarse cough but he held up a hand as she took a hesitant step towards him. 'Please go. Daniel will take you anywhere you want to go. I have work to do.'

Without another word, he walked up to the house

and the double cedar doors closed behind him. She was alone on the lawn, the champagne flutes winking mockingly at her as the fragile crystal fractured the afternoon sun into rainbows. She felt a tremendous urge to smash the crystal to bits, as Midas had just smashed her chances of getting Georgina back.

The fantasy was over. In a few minutes, the pilot would fly her back to Sydney and she'd have to confess her failure to Bill Downey. He would assign Jeff Pullen to the story and Jeff would pull his usual rabbits out of hats to win the sub-editor's job. Nice try, she told herself bitterly. She wasn't cut out for this kind of journalism. If it weren't for Georgina, she would give the whole rotten job away.

'Would you care for some more champagne?'

Lost in thought, Jill was startled when a middle-aged woman spoke beside her. The woman wore a coral-coloured jumpsuit which looked to be a uniform of some kind. 'No, thank you,' she said mechanically. As the woman began to clear away the tray, she added, 'Is there a telephone around here I could use?'

'There's one in the guest cabin.' The woman gestured towards one of the smaller buildings at the far end of the pool area. 'I'll show you the way.'

Putting the tray down, the woman led the way past the pool. 'I'm Stella Kimber, Mr Thorne's house-keeper,' she explained.

'Nice to meet you.' Jill's response was automatic. She felt ill equipped to deal with social niceties right now. She felt leaden and cold inside as she rehearsed what she would say to her editor. She wasn't looking forward to the conversation. Maybe she should post-pone it until she got back to Sydney.

But the housekeeper had unlocked the cabin and
stood aside to let Jill enter. 'The telephone is in the
main room,' she said.

'Thank you. I won't be long,' Jill said over her
shoulder.

'Take your time.'

With a friendly smile, Mrs Kimber withdrew,
closing the door behind her, and Jill heard her retrace
her steps around the pool. With scant interest, Jill
looked around. So this was where Midas accommo-
dated his friends. The word soured in her mind. She
was no longer a candidate for his friendship, and the
knowledge filled her with icy disappointment. In spite
of the odds against it, she had dared to hope that he
would understand her position. He hadn't even given
her a chance to explain. Well, it served him right if
Jeff Pullen got the assignment and tore his private life
to shreds.

The defiant thought brought her chin up and she
marched across the beautifully furnished living room
to the telephone visible on a low Tasmanian oak
coffee-table. Two deeply upholstered leather couches
faced each other across the table and there was a wall
of storage units housing every entertainment device
imaginable. A library of current films on videotape
took up another shelf. Midas certainly made his house
guests feel welcome.

Beyond the living-room was an equally inviting
bedroom with an enormous bathroom opening off it.
A small kitchenette allowed guests to help themselves
to snacks or coffee.

Tearing her eyes away from the surroundings, she
sat down and dialled Bill Downey's number. When

the long distance pips died away, she was put through to the editor, who sounded suspiciously jovial. The result of a long lunch, perhaps, or the expectation that her story was coming along well? She soon found out which it was.

'I've just come from a meeting with the publisher. I told him you were hot on the trail of his pet story.'

Her heart sank. 'He knows how difficult it is, doesn't he?'

'You know what Mr Savareid says about the impossible taking a little longer?' he observed, wariness creeping into his voice. He must have picked up the despair in hers.

'I know and I'm doing my best,' she hedged.

'Your best is a story on Gordon's desk,' he stated. 'You're not trying to tell me something, are you?'

'Such as what?'

'Such as you can't do it? Jeff Pullen is in my office right now and he's itching to have a crack at this.'

And at the sub-editor's job, she understood. A picture of her daughter's cherubic face filled her mind and her admission of failure froze on her lips. She couldn't let Bill give the story to Jeff. 'You can tell Jeff to find his own story. This one's mine,' she said grimly.

'Then you can deliver the goods?'

'Did you doubt it?' His voice had already told her he did. She felt the need to convince him even further. 'I'm calling from Vincero.'

There was an explosive outflow of breath down the line. 'You're where?'

'You heard me. I'm on Midas Thorne's private

island. He invited me here himself.' There was no
need to mention that he had already un-invited her.

'You *are* a fast worker.' Her editor's tone was filled
with admiration.

'Then you'll call Jeff off?'

Bill chuckled. 'You've got the assignment all to
yourself. Besides, I can't imagine Midas Thorne
inviting Jeff Pullen to Vincero, can you?' Almost as
an afterthought, he added, 'By the way, what colour
paint should I plan on ordering for your new office?'

Despair washed over her in waves. She'd done it
now, letting Bill think that the story was all but
written, when it was as far from her grasp as ever.
Keeping her misery out of her voice, she accepted
more unearned kudos from Bill and hung up. Her
mind whirled. Could she make a story out of what
she'd already seen? It was more than any other
journalist had ever done. It might be enough.

It had to be. Georgina's future depended on it. Jill
slipped her notebook out of her handbag and prowled
around the cabin, seeking the details which would
make her readers think she knew Midas Thorne more
intimately than she did—than anybody did. She
would stop short of actual untruths, but maybe she
could stretch reality a little. Her readers needn't know
that her description of Vincero had been gained as
she was being ignominiously expelled.

Although it was intended for a short stay, she could
live in the cabin, she decided. It had an airy quality
which appealed to her, from the lavish use of white
and yellow, to the summer lightness of the Monet
hanging in the main room.

The bedroom was equally bright, furnished in

white cane with a figured silk bedspread and matching drapes pulled back from floor-to-ceiling windows. They looked out on a view of the rain-forest and Jill smiled at the sight of a jewel-coloured parrot perching on a branch an arm's reach away.

It was a shame the windows at the back were sealed shut and the cabin air-conditioned. The forest would smell wonderfully fragrant, much nicer to wake up to than air-conditioning.

The view from the living-room and kitchenette was even more spectacular, taking in the pool area and the broad sweep of lawn down to the water's edge. The sheer beauty of it brought tears to her eyes. Georgina would love this place!

Thinking of her daughter renewed her sense of purpose and she filled her notepad with every detail she could glean from exploring the cabin, down to the kind of dinnerware filling the kitchen cupboards—Limoges china—and the designer swim-wear and bathrobes which hung in the dressing-room off the bedroom. Each garment came in several sizes, otherwise Jill would have suspected that they belonged to the woman in Midas's life. The strength of her reaction to this idea caught her off-guard, until logic told her the garments were kept here in case a visitor wanted to use the marvellous pool. Midas had thought of everything.

'Mrs Casey?'

Recognising the pilot's voice, she pulled the dressing-room door shut and slipped into the bath-room, calling out, 'I won't be a moment.' Then she flushed the toilet for effect and rinsed her hands, drying them on a fluffy Pierre Cardin towel. Her guilty flush was receding by the time she walked into the main room. 'I didn't hear you come in, Daniel.'

'Mrs Kimber told me I'd find you here. Mr Thorne put me at your disposal for the afternoon.'

'How kind of him.' Her thoughts raced as a plan began to form in her mind. 'I wasn't feeling too well and Mr Thorne thought I might want to fly back to Sydney. But I just telephoned my doctor and he suggested that rest is the best cure. I'm going to lie down here for a while.'

'I trust it wasn't the helicopter ride which upset you?'

He'd fallen for the first part of her story! She kept her sense of triumph in check. 'Of course not. It was wonderful. But I'm not a good traveller, I'm afraid.'

'Can I get you anything?'

'No, thanks. I'll be fine after a rest.'

'As you wish. I'll keep myself available until you're ready to leave.'

She gave a shy smile. 'Oh, that was only when we thought I would have to fly back. Now my doctor's reassured me, I won't be leaving at all tonight, so you needn't wait for me.'

The pilot looked uncertain. 'In that case, I'll check with Mr Thorne to be sure he won't need me again today.'

'He won't, I assure you. We'll be *much* too busy. I think you understand, don't you?'

Daniel Prasad looked acutely uncomfortable. He seemed torn between loyalty to Midas Thorne and a wish to stay out of his boss's love-life. She suppressed her elation. The pilot was totally convinced that she was Midas Thorne's latest dalliance, and Daniel couldn't wait to extricate himself. At the same time, she felt a twinge of conscience. She didn't like misleading the pilot, whose disapproval was obvious. But she was desperate. She couldn't leave until she had her story.

'Very well,' Daniel conceded. 'If you're sure Mr Thorne won't need me again today, I'll return to Sydney. I have things I must do there, so the extra time will be put to good use.'

'Are you married, Mr Prasad?' she asked on an impulse.

'Please, call me Daniel,' he insisted. 'I have a wife and four children, but they have yet to join me in Australia. They live in my home city of Nadi.'

She recalled that he came from Fiji. 'You must miss them.'

A coldness invaded his eyes but he smiled. 'Very much. We hope to be reunited soon.'

He gave a half-bow and left. His reaction puzzled her. All she had done was to ask after his family. She must be right. He disapproved of her supposed liaison with Midas Thorne. She wondered how he had come to work for Midas, and why his family hadn't accompanied him from the first.

None of it concerned her now, she reminded herself. She had achieved her aim of staying on Vincero. Now she needed to see more of the place. Realising what she'd done, she felt a little faint. It was the sort of thing Jeff would have done to get a story, but it was totally out of character for her. What would Midas think when he found out? It would confirm everything he believed about her profession.

It was too late to change her mind now. The

helicopter was taking off. Hearing the beat of the rotors, would Midas assume that she had left with the pilot? Her bridges were well and truly burned.

The next hour flew past. Keeping clear of the picture windows overlooking the pool, she finished her inventory of the cabin then made notes about everything she had seen since she got here, including the helicopter ride, and the label of the champagne she'd been offered.

She soon had several pages of trivia. And trivia it was, she acknowledged with a sigh. There was nothing of substance to tell her readers what kind of man Midas Thorne was. It was all superficial.

She chewed the end of her pen. She could add her own impressions, gleaned from their first meeting on the stairwell but she was oddly reluctant to write about it. It felt like an invasion of her privacy. She wanted to keep the moment special, she realised, not share it with millions of readers. But what else could she write about? This was supposed to be a profile of Midas Thorne, the man.

The floor around her feet was littered with wadded pages of notebook by the time her task was complete. Even achieving this much had exhausted her resources.

It was still afternoon. She couldn't venture outside until dark. What was she to do with herself until then? The king-sized bed beckoned and she decided to take a nap. She'd already refreshed herself with coffee and cheese biscuits from the well-stocked kitchenette.

Gathering up the debris of her notes, she stuffed the tell-tale signs into her bag and retreated to the bedroom, half closing the door in case anyone glanced into the cabin. She had tidied away all signs of her occupancy.

Tension throbbed through her as she stretched out on the bed. She felt what she was, an interloper in Midas's private domain. How he would hate her when he found out. As a journalist she shouldn't care but she was deeply troubled nevertheless. Midas had called her his friend. Friends didn't betray each other.

Relaxation came slowly as she deliberately slackened each muscle in turn. Her mind kept wandering to images of Midas beside her on the stairs, pointing out landmarks as they travelled here, and toasting her in champagne. She fell asleep with his face vivid in her mind.

It was no wonder she dreamed of him, but what disturbed her was the nature of the dream. He came to her, not in a business suit, but draped in a toga-styled garment, like a Roman senator. His patrician profile looked even more noble and his tan had deepened to a tantalising mahogany. Every sculpted muscle gleamed as he approached and she felt a yearning deep inside her, such as she had never known before.

'Oh, Midas,' she murmured, lifting her arms to him.

His eyes caressed her, molten with desire. 'Jill, my friend, my soul-mate.' He came closer.

Only then, she became aware that she was really hearing his voice but it was coming from outside the cabin. She struggled to wakefulness, surprised to find the room in darkness. She must have slept for several hours.

Cautiously, she slid her shoes on and moved into the main room, following the sound of men's voices. From behind the curtains she saw Midas and a group of men gathered on the lawn, only yards from her hiding place. The area was floodlit so brightly it might have been daylight outside. So much for her plan to snoop around the complex under cover of darkness.

Another man joined the group and she recognised him as Ted, Midas's security guard. A gleaming white launch was moored at the jetty. The men must have arrived by boat while she was asleep.

Straining to hear, she was unable to distinguish what the men were talking about. She caught several foreign accents and an occasional hint that they were discussing business. It must have something to do with the big announcement expected from Midas's company.

Eavesdropping on his business affairs hadn't been part of her plan when she'd decided to stay here uninvited, and she felt guilty for listening in now. But even if she ignored what was happening Midas wouldn't believe her, so she might as well hear the whole story and be damned for it. She would get the blame anyway, once he found out she was still here against his express wishes. At least this way, some good would come from her activities. Breaking the story of his new business deal would secure her promotion and Georgina's future once and for all.

Darn it, she couldn't hear a thing behind these thick windows. She moved to the door and opened it a crack. Nobody looked her way so she eased it wider.

A few words floated to her ears and she strained to put them into some sort of context.

They were discussing diamonds and a development which would revolutionise the mining industry. But what? She widened the crack a fraction.

Moments later, she froze in horror. Unbeknown to her, Midas had moved closer to the cabin and, just as she stifled a sneeze, he looked her way. His blue eyes bored into her and his body tensed with the shock of recognition.

She closed the door and leaned against it, her heart pumping wildly. He had seen her. Any moment now one of his security people would burst in and haul her outside. She had to do something and quickly.

Trusting that Midas would wait until his guests were safely inside before having her thrown out, she had a flash of inspiration. If she acted quickly enough. . .

Diving for the bedroom, she shed her clothes in frantic haste. Then she snatched one of the designer bikinis out of the dressing-room. A lightning glance at the tag showed her it was a little small but would probably do. She began to slip it on.

The bottom half was a snug fit, the black and silver knitted fabric moulding her hips as if it had been sprayed on. The bra posed more of a problem. The halter design tied at her neck, leaving her back bare. At the front, it plunged to a deep V between her breasts, barely containing their fullness. Normally she would have discarded the suit as much too revealing but there was no time to choose another.

Taking a deep breath she stepped over her scattered clothes and returned to the main room, where she

fixed a bright smile on her nerve-taut lips, and threw
the front door open.

As a diversion, it was a masterpiece. In unison, the
men turned towards her, their eyes starting from their
heads as she emerged. She was uncomfortably aware
of the murmurs and low whistles which greeted her
arrival but she ignored them and headed straight for
Midas.

He looked as if he was about to explode. Although
his face remained impassive—his features carved out
of stone—his eyes blazed with anger. It was like
staring into the heart of a volcano.

Her steps faltered as she came closer but she forced
herself to go on. 'Midas, darling. You don't mind if I
take a dip while you're busy, do you? These endless
meetings make me so-o sleepy. Or else it was all that
champagne. I went out like a light after lunch.'

Linking her arms around his neck, she kissed him
full on the lips, to the appreciative murmurs of his
guests. Midas hardly moved. It was like kissing a
marble statue. All the same she felt an odd stirring
deep inside her, as if she had touched a live electrical
connection. She drew back, her eyes wide with
apprehension.

'Go ahead, have your swim—darling,' Midas said.
There were questions in his eyes, too, although they
were immediately eclipsed by his anger.

She needed no further urging. Praying that the
water was heated, she moved to the edge of the pool
and dived cleanly into the water. It was blissfully
warm and she began to swim laps, not daring to look
up to see what Midas was doing.

Just as she went into a tumble turn, a German-accented voice reached her ears. 'You're a dark horse, Midas. You didn't tell us that entertainment would be laid on.'

'It isn't.'

The other man misread the chill in Midas's tone. 'Hands off, eh? Well, all I can say is, welcome back to the land of the living. It's about time.'

She kept up her rhythmic stroking and breathing as the voices faded in the direction of the main house. He must have meant her to hear because Midas's voice carried on the night air. 'Ted, ask Mrs Casey to join me in my office when she finishes her swim. I'll expect her in five minutes.'

The steel in his voice brooked no argument. For the first time, she felt fear at what she'd done. At the same time, there was a sense of triumph. How could Midas throw her out now, without explaining her sudden departure to his associates? Of course, he could invent something about sending her to visit her sick mother, then put her on the launch back to the mainland. She was in his hands now and the thought of facing his anger turned her blood to ice.

The security guard crouched down at the edge of the pool, a towel spread in his hands. 'You'd better come out now, Mrs Casey. Mr Thorne is waiting for you.'

Climbing out, she allowed herself to be swathed in the blanket-sized towel. The night air was cool and she shivered, but whether it was from cold or the coming confrontation, she wasn't sure.

'You asked for it,' she told herself as she clutched the towel around herself and followed Ted up to the house.

CHAPTER FOUR

A TRAIL of wet footprints marked her passage down a wide, tiled hallway which ran the width of the ground floor. She gained an impression of a luxurious home which was nevertheless warmly enveloping. Big panelled windows were swathed in swag velvet curtains, and nineteenth-century-style carpets covered the glossy wooden floors. Hand-tinted lithographs, tapestries and original paintings decorated the walls.

Midas's study was on the ground floor, although 'study' hardly described the massive room in which Ted deposited her. There was no sign of Midas.

Still shivering, she went thankfully to the fire crackling in the huge marble fireplace. In front of it were two chintz-covered settees and a Georgian style coffee-table. Beyond that was a grand old Australian cedar desk littered with papers and computer spreadsheets. A computer looked out of place on a credenza. This must be where Midas worked when he was at Vincero.

'What the hell do you think you're playing at?'

At the sudden attack, she spun around, clutching her towel when it threatened to fall. A damp patch darkened the Persian rug beneath her feet. 'I have no excuses,' she said. 'I knew you were going to have me thrown out so I acted on impulse to stop you.'

'Which doesn't explain why you're here at all. I thought you left with Daniel hours ago.'

'You mustn't blame Mr Prasad,' she said hastily, afraid that he might think this was the pilot's fault. 'I told him you'd invited me to stay the night.'

She could hardly meet his withering gaze. 'Did you, now? All the same, he should have checked with me before taking your word.'

'He wanted to, but I gave him the impression that you and I, that we were. . .' She couldn't go on.

'Lovers?' She nodded. 'No wonder Daniel didn't want to consult me. You probably embarrassed the hell out of him.'

So Midas didn't make a habit of entertaining women at Vincero. The discovery provoked a quite unwarranted *frisson* of pleasure but she dismissed it. What did it matter if he kept a harem here? 'I'm sorry I misled him,' she said primly.

Midas's eyebrow lifted. 'But not sorry that you stayed under false pretences?'

Her eyes begged him to understand. 'I had to do it. So much depends on this story. On what I make now, I haven't a hope of regaining custody of my daughter.'

He raked long fingers through his hair, leaving spiky trails. 'You people think the end justifies any means, don't you?'

He was lumping her in with the hated journalists who had hounded his wife and child to their deaths. If he had slapped her, she wouldn't have felt more humiliated. 'I can't help what you choose to think of me and I don't care.' She recognised the lie as soon as it passed her lips. 'But I do care what happens to my daughter. Can't you understand that?'

'I understand that she has a scheming, conniving

woman for a mother,' he said in clipped tones, his words raining down on her like physical blows. 'Maybe the court knew what it was doing, giving custody to her father.'

'You bastard!' Provoked beyond endurance, she launched herself at him, wanting only to wipe the smugness off his handsome face. What did he know about a mother's love? Or about her ex-husband's character? If he knew Terry, he would never suggest such a thing, never. Her fists slammed against his shoulders in impotent rage. 'How dare you judge me? Look what happened to your own family!'

'By fury, woman, shut up!'

His hands clamped around her wrists and he dragged her upright, holding her a few inches away from him. She had never seen a man so incensed. There was murder in his eyes. 'I'm sorry, I didn't mean to say that,' she whispered, horrified at her loss of control. But the damage was done.

'You're despicable,' he ground out. 'How could I ever have thought I was attracted to you?'

Knowing that he *had* been attracted to her was unbelievably painful, as was the realisation that his feelings had died at birth. She slumped in his grasp. 'Please forgive me. What you said about Georgina belonging with Terry. . .it made me crazy. I've asked myself over and over whether it could possibly be true.'

His glittering gaze tore into her. 'Is it?'

She chewed her full lower lip before answering. 'No. Terry's totally selfish and a womaniser. I can't make myself believe that Georgina's better off living with him.'

'And you're a perfect role-model for her, aren't you?'

Her head dropped to her chest. 'You must know the answer to that already. I'm just doing the best I can, although it hasn't been worth much up to now.' She tried to straighten and relieve the tension on her arms which had begun to ache. 'Let me go, please. I'll get dressed and you can send me back to Sydney.'

'Not so fast,' he cautioned her. 'You may have got what you came for, but it leaves me with a serious problem.'

'What kind of problem?'

He released her at last and stalked to the fireplace where he leaned against the mantelshelf, staring into the flames. 'My business associates think you're my live-in lover.'

Rubbing her wrists which bore the livid marks of his fingers, she nodded. She had all but forgotten the other men. 'Will it matter if they find out that I'm really a writer who sneaked in here uninvited?' she asked. How damning it sounded!

'It will to me,' he said, his explosive tone startling her. 'They know I distrust the media. Before they came here they agreed to my rule that there would be no publicity about the project until I authorised it. Finding a journalist here will raise questions I have no intention of trying to answer.'

Her hand covered her mouth. Recalling what she'd overheard about a deal which could revolutionise the mining industry, she was horrified at the damage her rash act might have caused. 'What can I do?' she asked unhappily. 'It's too late to undo the impression I created out there.'

'Precisely.' His lip curled into a sneer. 'That's why you're going to finish what you started.' He moved towards her, his strides purposeful. 'You're going to keep on posing as my lover until this conference is over.'

Stunned, she stared at him. She wanted to make amends but he was asking too much. Her thoughts whirled. 'I can't. I'm no actress.'

'You put on a convincing show at the pool when you put your arms around me and kissed me.'

'That was different.' Desperate to avoid her fate, she had kissed him without giving herself time to think. 'I couldn't do it again.'

'Why not? Am I so repulsive to you, a man who can't even protect his own family?'

The colour bled from her face. 'No! I've apologised for suggesting any such thing. It was said in anger. I didn't mean it.'

He shook his head as if to dispel a powerful memory. 'It's not the issue now. What matters is what my associates think you're doing here. If you play along, I'm prepared to sweeten the deal for you.'

She was genuinely baffled. 'Sweeten it? How?'

'If you agree to play your part, I'll give you the interview that means so much to you.'

His deal must be vitally important to wring such a concession from him. She could imagine how difficult it must be for him to make the offer. Temptation warred inside her. If she accepted, she would have the story of the decade and every chance of getting Georgina back.

Still, she hesitated. By accepting his terms, she would confirm everything he believed about her profession, assuming she could carry it off. 'How can I act as if we're lovers when we don't even like each other?' she asked in despair.

'You'd be surprised.' He moved closer and removed the hands she'd pressed over her eyes. He was going to kiss her, she realised with a sudden adrenalin rush. He was only trying to persuade her. It didn't mean anything. So why did her body respond with instant arousal at the mere thought of his mouth on hers? Her muscles tensed as he lowered his head towards her.

'Relax. Think of it as a rehearsal,' he murmured.

There was no time to think of anything as he pressed his lips against hers and her mouth caught fire. Flames of sensation raced along her veins, heating her to her core. The blood began to throb at her pulse points and she closed her eyes as weakness assailed her. He was an expert lover, arousing her with the skill of a virtuoso. Lifting sensation-drugged eyes, she surprised a softening in his face which was at odds with his earlier coldness.

'Still think you can't do it?' he asked in a strangely languid tone.

'I. . . I don't want to,' she dissembled, shaken by the intensity of her reactions.

'But you will, won't you?'

'Yes.' Was that her voice, giving assent to his crazy proposition? His satisfied smile confirmed it and apprehension gripped her. 'It's only pretence though,' she said, as much for herself as for him. 'I mean, we only have to *look* as if we're lovers, don't we?'

'You want to know how far I intend to take this charade?' he asked. 'How far would you like it to go?'

She was rocked by the answer she found herself wanting to give. She didn't want him to make love to her for real, did she? This was only to get them both out of a difficult situation. 'I'll do whatever's necessary to keep my part of the bargain,' she said, fighting a sense of panic. How far *would* they have to take this? How far did she want it to go?

'Of course,' he murmured. 'Journalists always do what's necessary to get a story, don't they?'

Was that what he thought she was doing? Her response to his kiss had been so unexpected that the story hadn't crossed her mind. Surely he didn't think her capable of faking such a powerful response? It underlined his low opinion of her. She twisted free and crossed to the fire where she stood hugging her arms around herself. 'This isn't going to work.'

'It will if you want it to. You did it before when you pulled your Cinderella act on the stairs. Why not now?'

'It was no act,' she insisted. 'What's the use? I'll never convince you that you're wrong about me.'

'You don't have to. You only have to convince my associates that you're my mistress.'

A curious light came into her eyes. 'If I don't?'

'You may find that transport back to Sydney is impossible to obtain.'

'You mean you'll *make* it impossible.'

'I'll be too preoccupied with business matters to give it a thought.'

Her eyes widened. 'You can't keep me here against my will.'

'Who says it's against your will?'

He was right. Too many people had seen her performance at the pool. If she telephoned the police and accused Midas of keeping her here, who would they believe—Midas with all his power and influence, or her? The answer was depressingly obvious. 'Very well, I'll do it,' she capitulated. 'But I want your word I'll get my story before I leave.'

He regarded her coldly. 'I don't usually need to give my word twice on the same matter. You'll get your story, for all the good it may do you.'

'It will do Georgina a world of good,' she said, sensing that it would be in direct proportion to the harm it did her with Midas. There was no hope of their ever being friends now. She found the idea disquieting.

She slid two fingers under the waistband of the bikini to ease it. As it dried, it was cutting into her flesh. 'What shall I do about clothes and toiletries?' she asked. 'I'm not equipped for a long stay.'

'You'll find a satisfactory selection of clothes upstairs. The bathrooms are well stocked with toiletries. If you write out a list of anything else you require, I'll have Daniel bring it out with the morning mail.'

'Even though there's no transport back to Sydney for days?' she couldn't resist asking.

His face remained impassive. 'The helicopter is needed for more pressing errands.'

She ignored the jibe. 'How long do I have to stay?'

'My business should be concluded in a few days, a week at most.'

Her thoughts raced. Even a week would give her

plenty of time to write her story and turn it in. The
promotion would be hers within a fortnight. The
prospect lifted her flagging spirits. A week wasn't
forever. 'There's one more thing,' she said tenta-
tively. 'I usually call my daughter each night before
she goes to bed.'

He gave a non-committal shrug. 'Call anyone you
wish, other than your newspaper.'

Annoyance rippled through her. 'Would I do that?'

His cynical glance said he thought she would do
anything she considered expedient. She tried to tell
herself his opinion of her didn't matter. It didn't, did
it?

'I have to get back to my guests,' he said abruptly.
'Mrs Kimber will show you to your room and you
can change before dinner.'

Her startled gaze met his. 'Tonight? Can't I just
have something sent to my room?'

'Hardly. The others are agog to meet you.' His
tone said he didn't share their enthusiasm. 'We may
as well start as we mean to go on.'

He touched an intercom on his desk and summoned
the housekeeper. Shortly afterwards the woman came
in, masking any surprise she felt at seeing Jill still
there and scantily clad in a damp bikini. Her reaction
confirmed Jill's impression that Midas didn't make a
habit of entertaining women at Vincero. What would
have happened if she hadn't been a journalist? He
had been happy to invite her here before he'd found
out.

So busy were her thoughts that Mrs Kimber was
throwing open the door to a bedroom suite before Jill
had time to adjust to her surroundings. 'You'll find

everything you need in the dressing-room and the bathroom,' Mrs Kimber assured her, then left her alone to explore the suite.

The bedroom was of ballroom-sized proportions, with a view of the garden and the river. The bed featured a chintz-covered headboard and matching bedspread and curtains. Small touches like a jug of iced water with a twist of lemon on the nightstand added to the room's charm. Three doors opened off it.

The first door led to a dressing-room. A selection of brand new women's clothes hung on a rack down one side. A rack of men's clothing filled the other side. With a jolt, Jill recognised the pin-striped suit from her first meeting with Midas. Surely he didn't expect her to share a dressing-room with him? There was another door at the far end of the small room. It must lead to his bedroom. She tried the handle but it was locked.

Returning to the bedroom, she opened the second door, revealing a spacious en-suite bathroom complete with deep claw-footed bath, brass fittings, and a wicker basket piled with fluffy white towels. There was a selection of toiletries on a wicker shelf above the washstand.

Since Midas expected her to join him for dinner, she reserved further explorations for later and began to run a hot bath. The tub took some time to fill so she busied herself selecting an outfit from the dressing-room. Whoever chose the garments for Midas had excellent taste, she thought as she tried an embroidered top against herself. Part of a two-piece suit, it had a scoop neck, scalloped edging and cap sleeves.

The full skirt was elasticated at the waist with more embroidery around the scalloped hemline. The shop tags were still attached and she removed them.

There were drawers full of exquisite silk underwear in several sizes, so she had no trouble outfitting herself, although she was a little bemused to find such delicate things in a bachelor's quarters. Maybe he had a sister, or a girlfriend after all. The possibility was more trying than she cared to admit.

After a lingering rose-scented bath, she dressed in the lovely clothes, feeling a bit like a courtesan preparing to pleasure her master. She chided herself for letting her imagination run riot. Even if the cage was somewhat gilded, she was a virtual prisoner here. Somehow, the thought wasn't as disturbing as it should have been.

She was brushing her hair when a knock came on the door. It was Mrs Kimber. 'I've brought your things from the cabin,' she said, holding them out.

Seeing her clothes freshly pressed and her shoes cleaned, Jill flushed guiltily. What did the house-keeper think, finding Jill's clothes scattered across the floor of the cabin? Her expression gave no clues. 'Thank you,' Jill said, taking the clothes. On impulse, she asked, 'By the way, did you choose the lovely things in the dressing-room?'

The housekeeper shook her head. 'It was Mrs Fleming, Mr Thorne's sister. She's a dress designer,' she added.

No wonder the clothes were so exquisite. Jill had admired Kirsty Fleming's designs for a long time, not knowing that she was Midas Thorne's sister. Her store of information about him was growing all the time. Even as she assured the housekeeper that she had everything she needed, her mind raced ahead. If she could only survive these few days posing as Midas's mistress, her article would be sensational.

She found her way down to the dining-room by trial and error. Midas and his associates were waiting for her and their conversation died away, replaced by curious looks as she joined them.

A tall, broad-shouldered man with a blonde crew-cut, offered his hand. 'Miss Casey? Midas was telling us about you. I'm Gerhardt Muller.'

She took his hand and he bowed over her fingers. From his accent, he was the one who welcomed Midas 'back to the land of the living'. What had he meant by that?

There was no time to dwell on the question. Midas moved between her and Gerhardt Muller, introducing her to his other associates. There was Mr Yamamoto from Japan and Robert Waya from Fiji. She greeted them both pleasantly and allowed Midas to seat her on his right at the table.

During dinner, the conversation flowed around her as the men discussed international business affairs. Every now and then, out of deference to her, the subject was changed, but she had the feeling that the cut and thrust of business was what really interested them. She felt cross with Midas for insisting that she join them.

By the time they reached the coffee and port stage, she was worn out. Thankfully, the visitors apologised and retired early, having flown in from their various countries only that morning. 'Shall we have an early night, too, darling?' Midas asked her pointedly.

Her face became heated and she gritted her teeth, but made herself say pleasantly, 'Of course, darling.' It sounded so forced that the others must notice. But they exchanged looks of frank envy with Midas as they said their good-nights.

'You'll have to do better than that,' Midas said in an undertone, as he escorted her to her room.

Outside the door, she turned to him. 'It's difficult, when I know how much you dislike me.'

He held the door open for her. 'It's your job I dislike, not you.'

Her glance was withering. 'You needn't pretend something you don't feel. I'll brush up my act without any false encouragement from you.'

'Of course.' The dark eyes froze with contempt which, although hurtful, was at least believable. Anxious to be alone, she slipped through the partly open door.

She was stunned when he followed her, closing the door behind him. 'What do you think you're doing?'

'Turning in. What does it look like?'

'But this is my room.' She remembered the men's clothes in the dressing-room and shook her head wildly. 'Oh no, I didn't agree to carry the charade this far. I insist on having a room to myself.'

'You're in no position to insist on anything,' he reminded her coolly. 'You'll do whatever I deem necessary to uphold your end of the bargain.'

Her eyes widened. 'That doesn't include sleeping with you.' Her denial held a hollow ring which he recognised, she saw by the swift flare of interest in his eyes. 'You can't mean to tell me that the success of your deal hinges on whether or not your friends see us sharing a room?' she implored.

'I couldn't give a damn what they think,' he said dismissively. 'This saves me the trouble of explaining myself to anyone. Besides, it's time you found out that when I do something, I do it very thoroughly indeed.'

How thoroughly? she wondered as her heart raced like an express train. She slid damp palms down the sides of her dress. 'All the same, I don't make a habit of sleeping with my interview subjects,' she denied.

'You did once.'

It was said so matter-of-factly that it took her a moment to digest. Since unmasking her, he must have checked into her background. 'I was married to Terry Casey,' she said diffidently.

'So that's how you operate,' he said with deceptive mildness.

Her head snapped back. 'What do you mean?'

'You use your favours as leverage,' he went on. 'Well, it won't work with me. I have no intentions of offering you marriage so I can sleep with you, only of sharing a room for my own convenience.' He strode past the bathroom to the third door and opened it. She found herself looking into a cosy sitting-room furnished with bookshelves and a velvet-upholstered day bed.

She felt foolish. This was where he had planned to sleep all along and had goaded her into defending her honour out of sheer bloody-mindedness. She masked her annoyance. 'Will you be comfortable there?'

He shrugged. 'It's only for a few days. I've endured rougher conditions back home in Tasmania.'

Her curiosity was piqued. 'You were poor as a child, weren't you?' The information came back to her from the newspaper files.

He nodded. 'We were dirt poor. I was born in a logging camp. But my family was rich in everything which mattered, things like love and trust. We're still very close.'

Jealousy threaded through her. After her own parents separated, they had pulled her back and forth between them like a puppet on a string. Love and trust were at a premium in her family. 'You bought your home town, didn't you?' she asked, recalling that it was now a monument to the timber pioneers, run as a tourist attraction by his parents. They were fiercely loyal to Midas, steadfastly refusing to sell the family secrets to the media, although vast sums of money had reputedly been offered. It seemed as if love and trust did prevail where he came from.

Midas made an impatient movement. 'There'll be time for the interview later. It's been a long day.'

He thought she was probing his background for the story, she realised unhappily. Hadn't he considered that she might want to know more about him for herself? 'I wasn't thinking of the story,' she said crossly.

His eyebrow arched. 'You can't be interested on your own account. Isn't there a journalistic code of ethics which forbids you to see me as a human being?'

'Go to hell.'

'After you,' he said magnanimously. Mocking lights flashed in his night-dark eyes.

For a moment, their gazes locked and the world seemed to spiral in on itself. Sounds were magnified.

His breathing oddly laboured; hers struggling to escape from a closed throat. The murmur of the air-conditioner. Distant voices outside somewhere. A faint sound which she recognised as her own thudding heart.

He took a step towards her and she held her breath, reliving in a flash the intoxicating feel of his mouth crushing hers. Hunger swelled inside her, but it couldn't be for a repeat of the experience, could it? She couldn't, wouldn't let it be so. Yet she was unable to tear her eyes away from him.

Then the spell shattered as Midas took a deep breath and released it slowly. His eyes telegraphed his contempt, before the lids came down. 'Don't you have to call your daughter? She's the reason you're here, after all?'

Her own reactions had so alarmed her that she spoke, more to convince herself than Midas. 'Georgina means more to me than anything else in the world. Anything.'

He nodded stiffly. 'Then call her. You won't mind if I use the bathroom first?'

Reminded of her purpose here, she banished the vivid images which rose in her mind, of Midas bathing, towelling his superb body, with no more than a span of timber separating them. She inclined her head. 'It's hardly my place to mind what you do here, is it?'

The speculative look he gave her made her wonder if he was reading more into the remark than she had intended. But he said nothing. By the time she had stilled her shaking fingers sufficiently to dial Terry's number in Sydney, Midas had shut himself in the bathroom.

After a few minutes of Georgina's childish chatter, Jill's sense of balance was restored. She knew why she was here and what she needed to achieve. Her all too human reactions to Midas were purely the responses of any healthy woman to a handsome, virile man. Chemistry, that was all.

The assurance didn't help her to banish him from her thoughts so she could get to sleep. Long after he emerged from the bathroom and went into his own room, closing the door, his image dominated her mind. It was almost dawn before she fell into a restless sleep.

CHAPTER FIVE

THE Hawkesbury River was a shimmering avenue between skyscraper peaks cloaked in green. A line of poetry by Matthew Arnold drifted into Jill's mind, '. . . The Majestic River floated on, out of the mist and hum. . .' A few remnants of morning mist still clung to the river, although it, too, would soon be burned off by the sun. An honour guard of seagulls lined the edge of the private jetty.

Already she loved being at Vincero in the mornings, when the mist lay like soft fleece over the water and the island rose like Brigadoon out of nothingness. As the sun travelled higher in the sky, the river's brilliance increased and it was soon hot enough to sunbathe by the pool.

The metallic silver bikini she was wearing was the same one in which she'd first posed as Midas's lover. Reluctant to put it on again because of this significance, she had tried several others and finally returned to this one. It wasn't a good fit but it was better than any of the others. Her breasts swelled over the tops of the bra cups, but there was no one to see her. Midas and his associates were inside, deep in the business discussions which had occupied them since they arrived. She could have sunbathed out here in the nude for all the attention they would have paid her.

A shadow fell across the paperback novel she was

reading and she looked up to find Gerhardt Muller looming over her. He was casually dressed in swimming shorts and a patterned shirt, open at the front. It was the first time she'd seen him in casual clothes and she was taken by surprise. 'Hello, Mr Muller. Meeting over?'

'It's Gerhardt, remember?' His tone rebuked her teasingly. 'And yes, the meeting is over. It is far too glorious a day to spend entirely indoors.'

'Which is why I came out here,' she agreed. She looked around but there was no sign of the others. 'Are you going to swim?'

'Soon, soon. First I shall soak up some sunshine and enjoy the view, which, if I may say so, is spectacular.' His German-accented compliment was directed at the river but his eyes lingered on the soft mounds of her breasts which strained her bikini top.

Instinctively she spread her book across her chest, earning a wry smile from Gerhardt. 'Is Midas joining us?' she asked pointedly.

'In his place, I would certainly do so,' the German commented, again managing to turn his remark into a compliment. 'This week hasn't been much fun for you, with us four tied up in meetings all day.'

An unexpected loyalty to Midas made her say, 'Not at all. How could I be unhappy when Vincero has so much to offer?'

And she hadn't. The last few days had been spent working on a children's story, Jill's first. Inspired by her nightly calls to Georgina, it was about a little girl and how she managed to deal with some bullies at her school. While Jill tried to make it entertaining in its own right, the story also contained ideas which she hoped other children would find helpful.

Midas had surprised her at work on the story the day before. When he found out that she wasn't writing her article, he wanted to know what was occupying her. Shyly, she had showed him, and been astonished when he'd said, 'It's very good. You have real talent.'

'Do you think so?'

'An essential attribute of a chief executive is the ability to spot talent and nurture it,' he told her.

She laughed. 'I don't know whether I have talent or not, but the nurturing part is easy in a place like this. Vincero is paradise.'

'It was Paradise Lost when I first saw it,' he said. 'The house was built in 1840 for a local magistrate. In the wine cellars you can still see the original chains and manacles attached to the sandstone walls. But it had been abandoned for years. The old convict-built barn was almost falling down.'

'You'd never know it to see it now.' Remembering that the place was accessible only by launch or helicopter, she was overawed. 'How did you get all the building materials up here?'

'The same way the pioneers did, by barge. The hardest part was excavating the pool out of the living rock. It had to be done by hand, to avoid disturbing the rain-forest and the native wildlife.'

'No wonder Vincero is special to you,' she observed. 'You put so much of yourself into building it.'

His velvet gaze caressed her. 'I believe that one

gets out of life only what one is prepared to put into it,' he said.

When had the atmosphere changed from friendly to something more intimate? It was like stepping off a sand bank you didn't know was there, and suddenly finding yourself in deep water. She floundered, out of her depth. 'That's a sensible philosophy, I suppose,' she stammered, aware of his eyes burning into her and the swift rise and fall of his chest as his breathing quickened. Sensing danger, she plunged on, 'In journalism, we say, "there's no such thing as a free lunch".'

At the mention of her trade, the softness vanished from his eyes and his mouth tightened into a grim line. 'Quite so. No doubt you'll quote me on it in your article?'

'I suppose so.' The change from warmth to coldness had come about because she brought up her profession, she was well aware. Yet she hadn't given the article any thought for days and her interest in Vincero's history was genuine, although she knew Midas wouldn't believe it. Besides, she would have to start on the article soon. Much more of this lotuseating and she would start believing she really was Midas's mistress, with nothing more pressing to do than look decorative.

Gerhardt was addressing her again and she dragged her thoughts back to the poolside. Drifting off into daydreams was another bad habit she had acquired since coming here.

'Mmm,' she said non-committally, hoping that it was a suitable answer to Gerhardt's question which she hadn't heard.

'Mmm-yes, or mmm-no?' he insisted.

Her brilliant smile begged his forgiveness. 'I don't know. What was the question again?'

'Why do I think there's a sharp brain inside that beautiful head of yours?' he mused. 'Pretending you didn't hear me invite you to my home is a clever way to avoid offending both me and your benefactor.'

So that was his question. 'I certainly don't wish to offend you,' she said sincerely, 'but Germany is a long way away.'

He shook his head. 'I was thinking more of Bellevue Hill than Bonn. I have homes in both places.'

As he named the wealthy Sydney suburb, apprehension rippled through her. He was coming on to her, right under the nose of her supposed lover. She can't have played her part very well if Gerhardt had gained the impression that she could be wooed away from Midas. 'I don't think Midas would like it,' she said firmly.

'You prefer to be lonely here with him?' Gerhardt sounded disbelieving.

Strangely enough, she did. Gerhardt would spoil her outrageously, seldom leaving her alone as he thought Midas did. Yet, had she been Midas's mistress for real, she would still have preferred him to Gerhardt. It was true that she hadn't seen much of Midas, except in the evenings. But she was self-sufficient and didn't mind. There was plenty to occupy her. She didn't need to be constantly amused like a child.

Rather than resent the business activities going on around her, she had become curious. What project could involve people from such diverse backgrounds?

From snippets she'd already picked up, she gathered that Gerhardt's involvement was financial. He represented a banking group of some kind. She had no clues about Mr Yamamoto, although she assumed he would provide technological support. She had heard Midas conversing with him in Japanese, and concluded that he didn't speak very much English. Robert Waya, the Fijian, was more of a challenge. She knew that gold-mining was one of Fiji's main industries, and guessed that this was where he came in.

Gerhardt chuckled. 'You have a most quizzical expression on your face, little one, as if there was something you wanted to ask but dared not. Why not try me?'

Why not, indeed? 'I was wondering what project brings you and the others to Vincero.'

His indulgent smile irritated her. 'I dare say Midas wouldn't want to trouble you with such matters.'

Her anger rose and red patches coloured her cheeks. 'Please don't patronise me. I'll have you know I'm a. . .' Her voice tailed off. She went cold, realising how close she'd just come to giving herself away.

'You were saying?'

'I was saying that I'm pretty good at business myself,' she dissembled.

He patted her hand, encircling her wrist before she could snatch it away. 'I'm sure you're very competent,' he agreed. 'But it would be a sin to waste you in a boardroom when you could so enhance a bedroom.'

To her horror, his hand dropped to her leg and he skimmed it with light fingers. It could have been an accidental contact, as he withdrew his hand, but she was sure it wasn't. He wanted her and he wanted her to know it. What would Midas think of his business partner now? Or were they so used to pooling their corporate resources that the habit extended to their private ones as well?

Her doubts were dispelled when Midas appeared at the poolside. Under his searching gaze, Gerhardt jumped away from her as if burned but recovered his composure quickly. 'Your charming companion was taking an interest in our business.' He made it sound as if the whole scene was her fault.

Midas's frown told her he thought it was too. But his manner was lover-like as he dropped on to the lounger beside her and placed a hand possessively on her bare leg. The contact sent electric shivers of pleasure along her nerve endings, in contrast to her revulsion at Gerhardt's touch. Like Gerhardt Midas was casually dressed, in a pale blue Lacoste shirt and jeans. His dark chest hair teased at the open throat of the shirt and it was an effort to drag her eyes away.

His expression was anything but pleased. 'So Jill was worrying her head about our business? How many times must I tell you to let me take care of such matters.' His indulgent tone didn't disguise the steely thread of warning.

'You needn't worry, I didn't learn very much,' she said acidly. 'Gerhardt had other things on his mind.'

'No doubt.'

With alacrity, Gerhardt got to his feet. 'I'll leave you two alone.' Forgetting his intention to swim, he disappeared into the house.

The loving Midas vanished with him. The hand

which had been idly caressing her arm became a steel vice around her wrist. 'Now what the hell were you doing, flirting with Muller? Were you hoping to get information out of him for your story?'

Her breathing became ragged. It was so unjust that she wanted to cry. 'Hasn't it occurred to you that *he* might have been flirting with *me*?' she demanded.

'You didn't encourage him?'

'I was about to fight him off when you appeared on the scene.'

Some of the anger drained from his face and he looked thoughtful. 'Come to think of it, he *has* been overly attentive to you. Maybe I should have a word with him.'

'No, it would be my word against his.' She would hate to be responsible for damaging an important business relationship. It wasn't as if Midas genuinely needed to defend her honour. He was only concerned about appearances, although she had to admit that he was playing his part with extraordinary thoroughness. 'I don't want to cause any trouble,' she finished.

His gaze seared her. 'There's a first time for everything, I suppose.'

She felt driven to defend herself. 'I wasn't trying to get information out of Gerhardt,' she insisted. 'If you must know, he suspects that our relationship isn't all that it seems.'

His hand slid slowly, tantalisingly over her hand and travelled down the curve of her hip. 'Then we must work harder to convince him.'

A strangled breath escaped from her throat. He was only doing this to remind her of their bargain, but she found herself wishing that there were more to it. Good grief! She didn't actually want him to make love to her, surely? All she wanted was her story. Midas's reasons were equally cold-blooded so there was no point fantasising about anything else. His willingness to accuse her of seducing Gerhardt to obtain information was proof of his contempt for her.

Suddenly she became aware that he looked tired. Violet stains under each eye made him appear tougher than usual, although still ruggedly handsome. His business deal must be exacting a toll. 'Is the conference going well?' she asked.

'It's turning into more of a summit than a business conference,' he confided, surprising her. 'As well as juggling financial affairs, I have to balance Fiji's interests against those of Germany and Japan.'

'Your pilot comes from Fiji. Surely he can be of some help,' she suggested. She had expected Daniel to be pleased about the arrival of a fellow countryman. But when he delivered the items on her list, he had reacted angrily to her mention of Robert Waya. Giving no explanation, he had left her supplies and stalked away.

'Daniel's heritage is Indian. There's a lot of tension between his people and the full-blooded Fijians,' he told her.

'And Robert Waya is Fijian,' she concluded. 'It explains why they don't seem to get along.'

Midas nodded. 'I've kept them as far apart as possible. Daniel is a brilliant pilot, but his political views can't be allowed to interfere when jobs and futures are at stake.'

He had more on his shoulders than she imagined

and she felt a surge of sympathy for him. 'There must be a lot at stake,' she commented.

'There is.' He stood up. 'Perhaps it's time you knew precisely how much. Would you like that interview I promised you?'

Caught off guard, she blinked in astonishment. 'Right now?'

'We've broken for the afternoon. Matsuhiro is resting. Robert is sending faxes to his government. And we both know what Gerhardt is doing.'

Her colour heightened as she thought of what Gerhardt wanted to be doing and she scrambled to her feet. 'I'll go and get ready.'

'We'll go together. There's a tape recorder in the suite. We may as well record the interview there.'

It was out before she could stop herself. 'But if we go in now, everyone will think that we're. . .' She couldn't finish the thought.

He finished it for her. 'Exactly. They'll think we're making love. It's better than having them discover that you're really a journalist instead of my mistress.'

She couldn't fault his logic although it provoked an odd feeling of let-down. If it meant she got her story, and a chance at regaining custody of Georgina, she should be pleased with his subterfuge. Instead, she felt cheated. Did some part of her wish that they *were* going to make love? This method acting was danger-ous if she was starting to believe her own performance.

By now, the suite they shared was comfortably familiar. Except for the fact that they slept apart, it was almost as if they *were* a couple. They took turns using the bathroom, deferring to one another with exaggerated courtesy. They had even formed the habit of leaving personal items lying about.

Jill was no longer embarrassed at finding Midas's clothes hooked behind the bathroom door, or his after-shave lotion on the side of the bath. He had a habit of leaving the top off. Screwing it back on one morning, she'd lifted the bottle to her nose, breathing in the leathery scent which was so reminiscent of him, until she realised what she was doing and thrust the bottle into the cupboard.

She blamed the lapse on her own need to be part of a pair, which she acknowledged with difficulty. She simply wasn't the swinging single type. Marrying Terry had been a mistake but the length of time she took to undo it showed how much she wanted a man in her life. Not just any man, but someone she could love with all her heart. Having Midas around felt right, even though their relationship was a fiction. It was the way she wanted her life to be.

Midas closed the main door behind them. 'Get changed. I'll set up the recorder.'

Instinctively, she bridled. They were out of sight of the others now. He had no right to order her around. She was tempted to ignore his instructions and conduct the interview dressed in her bikini. At the same time, she sensed a tension radiating from him which warned her not to try him too far. Lately it had been all too easy to forget that she was here on assignment. Unable to take notes or do anything which would betray her identity, she had almost managed to forget how much Midas disliked what she did. Until now.

Now the game was over and she had a job to do.

But their imaginary relationship was so warm and pleasant that returning to reality came as a shock. With shaking fingers, she belted a silk robe over her bikini, afraid to hold Midas up now he was ready to proceed. She just wished he would stop looking at her as if seeing her for the first time. The woman and the journalist are one, she wanted to scream. How could he be so charming to the one and yet so bitter towards the other?

The tape recorder was a compact battery-operated model with a built-in microphone and Midas had set it up on a low table opposite the day bed where he slept. Each morning Mrs Kimber made it back into a couch and Jill wondered what the housekeeper thought of the situation. She never gave any clues.

With no other chairs in the room, Jill had no option but to share the couch with Midas, although she kept a wide swathe of velvet between them. In the small room he seemed larger somehow, more powerful. She wished she'd changed completely instead of putting the robe over her bikini.

With an effort, she marshalled her thoughts. 'We'll start with your background, how you got to be where you are today.' Her voice came out irritatingly husky and she coughed to clear it.

'Will we?' he drawled. 'Is anybody interested in my ancient history?'

'I. . .the readers,' she corrected herself, 'want to know what's behind a high achiever like Midas Thorne. It makes them feel as if they know you.'

'I'm not sure I want that many friends,' he growled. He looked as if he would like to end the interview here and now. His muscles were bunched as if for flight, and his jaw was set in a grim line. He reminded her of the tiger at Taronga Zoo, a vision of great power held in check with a mighty effort.

To encourage him to relax, she lowered her voice to a murmur as she asked about his early career. She learned that he had left Tasmania, at sixteen and worked in isolated mining towns on the mainland, studying in every spare moment until he achieved his dream of becoming a mining engineer. Arriving in Perth at the height of the nickel boom, he formed a syndicate and began buying control of private prospecting companies until, a decade later, he controlled a modest mining empire.

One of the company shells under his control had struck a fabulous diamond deposit, forming the basis of his present fortune.

'It's exciting stuff,' she observed, trying to encourage him to reveal more.

'There's nothing new in it,' he dismissed. 'I can't see you winning any awards with this story.'

Nor would she if he kept to the bare facts. Most of them she could have pieced together from articles in business journals over the years. 'I really want to know about the man behind the story,' she probed, and didn't correct herself this time. 'What makes you so success-orientated?'

For a moment, she thought he wasn't going to answer but her question had caught his interest. He steepled his fingers and concentrated his gaze on them. 'Power,' he said at last.

She felt a faint *frisson* of disappointment. Surely he wasn't after power for its own sake? 'Would you explain that?'

He switched his focus to her. 'When you're as poor as my folks were, you're vulnerable. I wanted the power to control my own life. Success gives you that power.'

Although she told herself that his motives, pure or otherwise, were nothing to do with her, a feeling of relief coursed through her. She would have been disappointed to discover that he relished power for its own sake. She ran an eye down her notes. 'You've certainly reached your goal. Ownership of your former home town, gold-mines, diamond-mines, cattle ranching. Is there anything you *can't* have?'

His eyes narrowed and his knuckles whitened as he clenched his hands. 'You of all people can ask me that?'

He was thinking of his loss and she cursed her own thoughtlessness. 'I'm sorry,' she said softly. 'I didn't mean to touch a nerve.'

He seemed to regret his harshness. 'Forget it. We can hardly get through a discussion of my personal life without mentioning that I had a wife and child.'

Lowering her head, she nodded as a tightness clutched at her throat. 'Your wife must have been proud of your success,' she ventured. 'I understand that you were married before you achieved all this.' Her gesture encompassed the island and all that is represented. 'Did success affect your relationship?'

'We were happy right up until the end,' he said shortly.

His anger was almost palpable. 'I didn't mean to suggest anything else,' she assured him.

His eyes blazed. 'Oh, no? You'd love me to admit that she couldn't handle our lifestyle, wouldn't you?

Then you could write that she was under stress when the baby was born. It would let the media off the hook nicely, wouldn't it?'

'I wasn't suggesting any such thing,' she said, never having considered the possibility. If *he* had, it would explain the force of his reaction to an innocent question. A tougher journalist would have pursued the point, she knew, but she hadn't the heart. She sighed. She would never win a Walkley award for her work at this rate.

He caught the whisper of her sigh. 'I promised myself I wouldn't bite your head off for doing your job, and here I am doing it. Let's try another question.'

There was no apology in his gaze. 'I know it must be difficult talking about yourself,' she conceded.

'I can handle the questions,' he said with an odd glimmer in his eyes. What did he mean? If her questions weren't the reason for his obvious tension, then what was?

And then she knew. As emotional thread wound between them, tangling her in its web, as understanding came. 'Is it because of me?'

His eyes probed her face, their intensity electrifying. 'What do you think?'

She didn't know what to think. Focusing on the interview, she had managed to ignore the signals passing between them, telling herself she was imagining them. He didn't want her. He didn't even like her. The tape recorder hissed between them like an accuser. So the powerful sensations sweeping over her couldn't be real.

Yet they were real. He felt them, too. An aching

sensation throbbed through her, heightening as her nipples peaked against the fabric of the bikini top.

He rose like a robot, his eyes glittering as they fastened on her flushed face. The movement of his Adam's apple as he swallowed caught her attention and she watched the small movement in fascination as he came closer.

When his arms enfolded her, she melted against him with a sigh. The heat of his body and his overwhelming maleness fired an answering warmth inside her. She shuddered as he pulled her hard against him.

His mouth was hot and urgent and his fingers twined in her hair with the ferocity of his need. Unheeded, the silk robe slid open and the cold metal of his jeans zipper imprinted itself on her skin. She hardly noticed. She could barely absorb each sensation before another took its place. She was drowning in a sea of them, swept away on a tide of pure feeling. Clinging to Midas was the only way to keep from going under.

The interview was driven from her mind as she gave herself up to the heady pleasure of being in his arms. Her lips parted and she gasped as his teeth grazed the sensitive inside of her lower lip.

She was unprepared when he lifted his head and said coldly, 'Is this for the article, too?'

Her hurt response was instinctive. 'No, of course not. For a moment I forgot. . .'

'That you're a journalist, the enemy?'

That she wasn't really his mistress and there was nothing between them but a cold, hard agreement made reluctantly on his part. Now he was reminding her of the painful truth.

In an agony of disappointment, she stepped back and pulled her robe around herself, fumbling as she tried to knot the belt. Before reminding her of her place, he had given her a glimpse of what it would be like to be loved by him. It was a taste of forbidden fruit and now he was reminding her that it *was* forbidden. 'Don't worry, I won't forget again,' she said stiffly, as much to herself as to Midas.

'You should have listened when I told you to change,' he said. 'Although if this is part of your interview technique, it's most effective.'

She turned away, hunching her shoulders. 'It isn't, but I don't expect you to believe me.'

There was no answer and the silence was broken by a click as he turned off the recorder which was still running. 'We'll finish this in my office,' he said crisply.

He was taking no chances on a repeat of what had just happened, she noticed. She nodded, not trusting herself to speak.

'Good. Come down when you're dressed. I'll be ready.'

He left, taking the recorder with him. Watching him go, she felt tears prickle the backs of her eyes as she relived the last few minutes. The pressure of his hands on her back and in her hair was all too vivid, as was the cold bite of his jeans fastenings against her fevered skin. For a moment she had allowed her feelings to carry her away, deluding herself that Midas wanted to give her the love she needed. How could he when she represented all that he hated?

By the time she joined him in his study she was composed again, at least outwardly. She had changed into the culottes and knitted vest she'd been wearing when she'd arrived. It seemed like a lifetime ago. Could it really be only a few days?

'Are you ready to continue?'

It was clear he meant the interview, that was all. She nodded, determined not to reveal her own confused feelings. 'I'm ready.'

As Midas began to talk about the deal he was orchestrating between his international partners, she knew she should feel privileged at being taken into his confidence. But it was an effort to keep her mind on the job, when it insisted on wandering to his powerful hands and imagining them splayed across her back. Or to listen to his words without feeling his sensuous mouth playing tunes of love on her parted lips.

She dragged her mind back to the present. 'You're *making* diamonds?' she said, as the sense of what he was saying caught up with her.

'Industrial diamonds for use in the mining industry,' he said in a tone which indicated he was repeating himself. 'You haven't been listening, have you? My company has patented a method of making industrial diamonds from carbon much more cheaply and quickly than it's ever been done before. The process will be worth millions to mining companies who no longer have to pour funds into replacing worn-out drilling equipment. The diamond coating can also be used in optical lens manufacture and polishing other diamonds.'

She listened, bemused, as he explained the process.

It seemed as if she would need a degree in physics to fully understand. She was thankful to have it all on tape, to be sorted out later. 'Aren't you concerned that I'll break the story before you're ready?' she asked when he finished.

He shook his head. 'By the time you leave the financial world will be informed, so you can't do any harm. This will save you the trouble of pumping the others for the details.'

She kept her gaze level although her eyes blurred. 'You don't think much of me, do you?'

'Not with millions at stake, as well as countless jobs and futures.'

He still didn't trust her. Had he kissed her to make the same point? She drew a strangled breath, feeling as if she had been punched in the stomach. Was Midas merely staking his claim on her after Gerhardt's intrusion? The evidence was there if she wanted to interpret it that way. In the interview, Midas had said that he was a territorial animal. Had Gerhardt encroached on his territory?

As she gathered her things to end the interview, he came up behind her and her body quivered with awareness. 'About this afternoon,' he began.

She kept her eyes averted. 'If you're referring to what happened upstairs, I'd rather forget it.' And forget her own wanton behaviour. Nothing good could come of it.

When she finally looked up, his face was an expressionless mask. 'If that's how you want it.'

She met his eyes unwaveringly, hating herself for the lie. 'Of course,' she said. How else could it be?

CHAPTER SIX

JILL didn't care if her absence caused comment. She was tired of posing as Midas's mistress. After coming so close to making the pretence a reality, how could she sit opposite him at dinner without reliving the power of his kisses and the passion of his touch? She couldn't hide in her room forever, but tonight wasn't too much to ask.

When she pleaded a headache Mrs Kimber was sympathetic, thoughtfully providing some aspirins with the tray she sent up. There were advantages to having staff, Jill reflected. Midas wouldn't find out that she was eating in her room until it was too late to do anything about it.

Playing back the tape of her interview with him was almost her undoing. The first part dealt with his early career but she'd forgotten that the tape had been running when he kissed her. The whole shameful incident was there, from her strained question, 'Is it because of me?' to the throaty sounds of his breathing as he enfolded her in his arms. In the evening stillness, the sounds were magnified and her pulses leapt as her mind conjured up the images which went with the sounds.

It was like listening to a radio play you knew had an unhappy ending. There was nothing she could do to change it, nor could she bring herself to fast-forward the tape past the damning moment when he remembered that she was a journalist. Her eyes were bright with tears by the time the tape clicked off, then on again as they resumed the interview in his study.

Desultorily, she began to outline the article, but the work was curiously unsatisfying. Bill Downey would be pleased with the material, but revealing Midas to the world gave her no pleasure. It felt like a violation. Maybe he was right. The public didn't need to know all about him. What was she doing pandering to their curiosity anyway?

Since coming to Vincero she had learned something important about herself. She wasn't cut out to be an investigative journalist. Leave that to the Jeff Pullens of the world. She was happiest working on the children's story she planned to dedicate to Georgina if and when it was published.

She chewed her pen thoughtfully. Perhaps she should try to make a career as a children's writer. Sure, and support herself with what? Once she regained custody of Georgina, she would need her job more than ever. Even then, supporting them both wouldn't be easy. Without the affordable child care provided by her employer, it would be nearly impossible. It was a depressing thought and a far cry from her ideal of motherhood.

Still, the thought was enough to make her buckle down to some serious work on the article. It was late and her wrist ached by the time the rough draft was written. With pages littered around her on the bedcover, she lay back against the pillows just for a moment, to rest her eyes.

She was asleep when Midas came in and found her,

her head dropped to one side amid a tangle of golden curls, her reading glasses sliding off the end of her nose. She looked like a child wearing her mother's glasses, he thought, coming to a halt at the foot of the bed. Jill was wearing the silk robe over a short lace-trimmed nightie which revealed her long legs, tanned honey-gold.

Telling himself that she would catch cold if he left her like this, he gathered up the hand-written sheets of paper, frowning when he saw what they were. Then he removed the glasses from her nose and put them on the bedside table.

At his touch, she stirred slightly, her lips softening into a Mona Lisa smile which made his heart feel as if someone was squeezing it in a vice.

He wanted to wake her and make love to her, he realised with a shock. He had wanted to do it this afternoon. What was happening to him? Hadn't he said himself that she was the enemy?

Almost of its own accord, his hand went out and he touched the backs of his fingers to her cheek. Her skin felt like satin. Before he could stop himself, he leaned over her and kissed her half-open mouth. She murmured in her sleep and he drew back, stunned at his own behaviour.

With jerky movements, he slid the bedcover out from under her and tucked it around her. Like a kitten, she snuggled under it, gripping the edges so only her fingertips showed. She didn't stir when he abruptly snapped off the light and stalked into the other room.

* * *

Next morning she awoke feeling light-hearted, then the reason came back to her. Last night she had dreamed of Midas. So vivid was the memory of his mouth on hers that she had difficulty in dismissing it as a dream.

With the main work of the conference behind them, Midas planned to take his associates out on the river in his cruiser, the *Lady Why*. When he broached the subject at the close of the interview, Jill had tried to exclude herself from the outing. The last thing she wanted was to spend a whole day in the confines of a cruiser with Midas Thorne, knowing that every touch and glance would remind her of the day before.

But he would have none of her excuses. 'The others will expect you to join us and so do I,' he said in a tone which ended the argument.

'They're supposed to think that I'm your mistress, not your Siamese twin,' she protested, but knew that the argument was already lost. What Midas wanted, Midas got. Their short association had already taught her that much.

They assembled on the lawn beside the jetty where the cruiser was already tied up, gleaming in the morning sunshine. Joining Midas, Jill noticed the helicopter parked on the grass. Daniel must have brought the morning mail while they were having breakfast. 'Is Daniel coming with us?' she asked Midas, watching the pilot inspect the sleek aircraft.

Midas glanced at the pilot. 'I doubt it. I have to order him to take a day off as it is.'

'He probably misses his family too much to enjoy his free time. Keeping busy might help,' she observed. 'He told me you're trying to arrange for his family to join him here.'

A frown etched Midas's forehead. His gaze swung towards Robert Waya who was engrossed in conversation with Gerhardt Muller on the deck of the *Lady Why*. 'I hoped this conference would help matters,' Midas said in lowered tones. 'I even made a few business concessions which could help, so maybe I'll have some good news for Daniel when this is over.'

'Have you told him?'

'Yes, but I cautioned him not to raise his hopes. The whole matter is politically sensitive.'

She nodded, recalling the wire service stories about the military coup which had rocked Fiji and the social upheaval which had followed. She had reported it without giving it a great deal of attention. Now that she knew someone who had been personally affected, she felt more involved. She made a mental note to look up the stories in the newspaper morgue as soon as she returned to work.

Matsuhiro Yamamoto joined them, giving his familiar smile and bow. Midas greeted him in Japanese and the two fell into conversation. Gradually, they made their way aboard the cruiser and headed out into the Hawkesbury River.

The *Lady Why* was unashamedly luxurious. Built in the 1930s, the vessel was panelled and furnished in solid, hand-polished mahogany. The upholstery in the saloon was plush rose velvet and doeskin and the floors were covered in thick Tiffany red carpeting.

Seeing her interest, the skipper, Jack Dyer, explained that the vessel had been owned by some of Australia's best-known entertainers. Used for some questionable activities during the Vietnam War years, she had been burned to the decks. Midas had purchased the vessel in 1981 and had her totally refitted with no expense spared.

A commotion on the rear deck attracted her attention and she hurried aft in time to see Mr Yamamoto haul in a huge wedge-shaped black fish which thrashed about on the deck until Jack Dyer came to dispatch it. 'It's a flathead, at least eight pounds,' he confirmed. Midas translated the news into Japanese and Mr Yamamoto grinned broadly, insisting on seemingly endless photos of himself and his catch. Promising to have the chef prepare it for dinner, Midas finally ended the photo session.

There were no more spectacular catches but the morning passed pleasantly enough. Not being a fishing enthusiast, Jill spent most of the time dozing in a deck-chair, soaking up the sun. She would miss this life when she went back to work. And not just the lotus-eating, she accepted. Midas had come to play a big part in her life, probably more than he had any business doing.

At lunchtime, Jack Dyer took them ashore in the cruiser's dinghy to where the crew had set up a barbecue on the foreshore. Soon the mouth-watering smell of frying steak and marinated prawns sizzling on a hotplate filled the air. Salads and French bread were produced from huge hampers, and they enjoyed the best meal Jill could remember eating. 'You look as if you're having fun,' Gerhardt observed, wandering over to join her on a sun-warmed rock.

She tensed, recalling their last encounter. 'Why

not? It's a beautiful day.' Her tone was carefully neutral.

He held up a hand in mock surrender. 'Relax. I came over to apologise for yesterday. I somehow got the wrong idea about you and Midas. I didn't think you would mind if I made my interest known.'

'How do you mean, you got the wrong idea?'

'There were times when you seemed almost unfriendly towards him. Today, though, I can see how wrong I was.'

What was different about today? she wondered. It was true that she was finally able to relax around Midas, telling herself that the charade would be over soon. She had joined in the euphoria of Mr Yamamoto's catch, and even responded with natural enthusiasm when Midas caught her around the waist and hugged her during the general celebrations. If her behaviour had convinced Gerhardt that she was Midas's lover, she should congratulate herself. But she couldn't subdue the sharp pang which lanced through her. Not for the first time, she found herself wishing that it *were* real.

When the lunch debris had been packed away and the wild kookaburras hand-fed on the last of the scraps, she stretched and stood up. 'Are we going back to the boat now?'

'I've arranged a treat for our guests first,' Midas announced. Out of the bush appeared a tall, angular-looking man with a mahogany tan which heightened the craggy lines of his face. He was introduced as a park ranger and he was going to take the visitors for a walk into the bush to see some of the Aboriginal cave paintings and carvings which were found all over the Hawkesbury region.

Jill had visited them as a child and recalled that some of the carvings were gigantic. Some of the petrogylphs were more than eighteen metres high, carved into the terracotta-coloured rock faces. She was sure the visitors would find them fascinating.

'Aren't you coming with us?' Gerhardt asked when she voiced the thought.

She wrinkled her brow. 'I have a headache from being in the sun too long. I think I'll go back to the boat and rest.'

'Then I'll come back with you,' Midas volunteered.

He was only doing it for show, to make it appear as if he cared about her welfare, she acknowledged. 'There's no need for you to stay, I'll be fine,' she assured him. Spending the afternoon alone with him wasn't part of her plans. She'd been hoping he would go with the others so she could gather her confused thoughts. Now her plan had backfired.

'The others will be fine with the ranger,' he said mildly, but there was a familiar edge of steel in his voice. 'I'll see you safely back aboard.'

There was nothing she could do except wait in the dinghy while he farewelled the walking party, then came back to take her across to the cruiser. The crew had already gone back with the remains of their lunch. At least they wouldn't be entirely alone.

But when they got back to the *Lady Why* there was no sign of Jack Dyer or the rest of the crew. 'They've probably taken the other dinghy and gone fishing,' Midas said when she commented on their absence.

A lump rose in her throat. 'You've given them the afternoon off?'

'Why not? Until the others return, there isn't much for them to do.'

Except stop her from being alone with Midas, she thought bleakly. She wished now that she had gone with the walking party. But she did have a headache from being out in the sun, although it wasn't as bad as she had made it sound. She decided to play it up now and hope that Midas accepted it.

Just knowing they were alone on the cruiser had put her senses into overdrive. It would be all too easy to let the boat's rocking motion lull her into believing the lie of their relationship. She touched a hand to her forehead. 'Would you mind if I lie down for a while?'

His concerned glance made her feel like a fraud. 'You really do have a headache?'

'Did you think I was lying about it?'

'No, but I wondered. . .hell, it doesn't matter. You can use my state-room. It's the most comfortable aboard.'

Comfortable was an understatement, she soon discovered. The lavish double bedroom was panelled in hand-polished mahogany and had thick-pile wool carpet underfoot. A round double bed dominated the floor space and a matching curved headboard, thickly velvet-padded, boasted a radio, cassette player and reading lights. An en-suite bathroom opened off the cabin and she was astonished to see a full-sized spa bath occupying one corner.

'Like it?' Midas asked, watching her eyes widen with amazement.

'It's positively decadent.' Surely he didn't spend all his time here alone? Who else had shared the round bed with him? It was none of her business, but the question bothered her all the same.

Midas went into the bathroom and returned with a glass of effervescent liquid. 'Soluble aspirin,' he explained, handing her the glass. 'Drink this, then lie down and your headache should disappear.'

She drank the medicine, wondering at the same time what the cure was for the turmoil inside her. It had nothing to do with the sun, and everything to do with being alone here with a man who very definitely turned her on. His closeness and the proximity of the vast bed were quickly turning the blood in her veins to liquid fire. Her headache was forgotten as dizzying waves of desire supplanted the pain.

She started when his hand brushed her arm but he was only guiding her on to the edge of the bed. When he dropped to his knees beside her and began removing her shoes, she stared at the sleek crown of his head, tempted almost beyond endurance to stroke the glossy strands to see if they felt as silken as they looked. Only when his hair slid between her fingers did she realise she had actually done it and then it was too pleasurable to stop.

As he eased her shoe off, his hand cupped her instep and he began to massage her toes, his thumb sliding sensuously across the tops. In some cultures the feet were the source of all pleasure and pain, and she soon found out why. When he removed her other shoe and transferred his attention to that foot, waves of shivery pleasure radiated up her calves.

Robot-like she moved her hand down the firm

column of his neck, the fine hairs at the nape teasing her palm. His breathing quickened and he looked up, his eyes fiery. 'Jill?'

Something in her face gave him the answer her voice refused to frame. With a groan of surrender, he buried his face against the soft mounds of her breasts. Her hands tightened on his shoulders, the muscles rippling under her fingers. Nothing mattered at that moment except the need to hold him as if she would never let go.

What they were doing was insane. They had different needs, belonged in different worlds. Yet not for the life of her could she summon the strength to push him away.

Neither did she resist when he unbuttoned her blouse and pushed it off her shoulders. Seconds later, her bra fluttered to her waist and he began to kiss her unfettered breasts. Her head dropped back and she closed her eyes as sheer ecstasy swept through her. His mouth was warm against her sun-dewed skin and she drew a strangled breath as his lips travelled along her collarbone and across her shoulder. Almost of their own accord, her hands crossed behind his head and she pressed him against the curve of her shoulder. The desire which gripped her was like a hunger, driving all other thoughts and needs from her mind.

'You know I want you, Jill.'

It was a statement rather than a question. There was no way to hide her response from him, nor his from her. 'We shouldn't,' she said, her voice vibrant with longings which contradicted her words.

'Of course not. We shouldn't do this.' He pressed his lips to the hollow of her throat. 'Or this.' He cupped her breast, bringing the hard nub of her nipple to his mouth. Flames raced along her veins and exploded deep in the pit of her stomach. He lifted his head and smiled at her. 'What else shouldn't we do?'

'We probably shouldn't make love,' she said, knowing that he was going to and she was going to let him. The discovery left her breathless with astonishment. She had never felt so on fire for a man in her life; had even entertained the idea that she might be frigid after the failure of her marriage. Yet now she blazed with a passion she was powerless to contain.

'Are you sure?'

'Are you?' Her molten gaze challenged him. Why should all the responsibility be hers?

His eyes were soft as they slid over her shimmering skin. 'I know I want to make love to you. I've wanted to since the moment we met.'

'On the stairs at the Sirius?' He nodded and her eyes shone with the delight of mutual discovery. 'I felt it, too.'

'And now?'

A lump rose in her throat, threatening to choke her. 'Now I don't know what I want any more.'

He gave her an angry little shake. 'Yes you do. We both know what we want. Say it, Jill.'

Mesmerised by his gaze which held her in thrall, she gave a little mew of defeat. 'Yes, I want you Midas. More than anything in the world.'

It was all the encouragement he needed. His breath escaped in an explosive sigh as he crushed her against him, raining kisses on her forehead and hairline while his hands roved over her shoulders and back.

When he released her to strip away his shirt with swift movements, she felt abandoned. But it was only momentary and when he claimed her again the teasing feel of his chest hair against her skin excited her anew, until she ached with the need to be part of him.

At first his touch was gentle as he caressed her until she cried aloud at the pure pleasure of his touch, wanting ever more closeness until she couldn't tolerate even the wafer-thinness of her bikini briefs coming between them.

As she struggled to kick them down her legs, he stood up and slid his jeans off, discarding the last of his clothing before he stretched out beside her. Now there were no barriers left.

All traces of shyness vanished and she began to explore his body as if it was an extension of her own, her sensitive fingertips tracing the steely rods of his bones under taut, bronzed skin. Every muscle and sinew yielded to her exploration and she twined her fingers in the dark curls of his body hair. Eddies of desire rocketed through her system. With a groan, Midas guided her hand lower and she gasped as her touch grazed the fullness of his manhood. Only then did she realise how tightly he had held his own desires in check for her sake.

His consideration brought tears to her eyes. He wanted her to be as ready as he was, before they made love. She had never dreamed that it could be like this.

Still he held himself back, his iron control evident in his shallow breathing and the flashes of red which stained his cheeks. With slow, sensuous strokes he massaged her stomach and thighs, heightening her desire until she thought she would explode with wanting him.

'Love me, please,' she implored, as every part of her thirsted for his possession.

'Still not sure?' he demanded, his voice a deep, passion-furred growl.

For answer, she clasped him to her, opening to him like a desert flower after rain. Her molten body flowed around him, making him part of her, his powerful maleness completing her, as if she had been a puzzle with a missing piece all of her life until now.

The moment of his possession brought her a peace and sense of rightness she'd never known before. Then she was swept along on a tide of such power and passion that she could no longer think or reason. She could only surrender to the kaleidoscope of sensations spinning her upwards and onwards, on a fantasy journey which seemed to last forever.

Her senses reeled as he carried her with him, slowly at first then with increasing urgency, until they moved as one towards a pinnacle of sensation which rocked her with its intensity.

She hadn't been alone on her journey, she saw as she opened misty eyes to gaze at him. The storminess was gone, replaced by velvety softness as he gazed down at her with heart-stopping tenderness. She had never felt so utterly loved in her life.

'This isn't real. I'm dreaming,' she said with a small shake of her head.

His laughter warmed her. 'If you are, we're having the same dream.' His hand on the satin curve of her thigh felt real enough and a shudder of remembered feeling surged through her.

His arm slid under her neck and she snuggled against his chest. Why had she been so afraid of letting him love her? The generosity of his love-making surely proved that he no longer held her profession against her. There was nothing else standing in their way.

Suddenly she needed to know the answer. 'Midas, tell me something.'

Drowsily, he nodded. 'You were wonderful, heavenly. Beyond my wildest dreams.'

Her laughter was slightly uneasy. 'I didn't mean that. I wanted to know what you feel about me, as a person.'

'Fishing for more compliments?' he teased.

'No. I just want to know that I'm accepted for. . .for what I am.'

'Why wouldn't you be?' His tone was wary.

'I'm still a journalist,' she said quietly, catching her breath as she waited for his response.

'You *were* a journalist,' he said firmly. 'Now you're my lover. Where's the problem?'

Her lower lip slid between her teeth and she chewed it thoughtfully. 'I don't know. I can't make a full time job out of loving you.'

'Well, you can have time off to sleep and shop.'

Instead of reassuring her, his teasing chilled her. Nothing had really changed, it seemed. They had become lovers but she had the awful feeling they still hadn't become friends.

'Be serious for a moment,' she insisted.

He linked his arms behind his head. 'I am being serious. All I want at this moment is to hold you in my arms.' He rolled over on to his side, resting his head on a bent arm. 'What do *you* want, Jill?'

She wasn't sure she knew the answer herself. The tangle of needs inside her ranged from acceptance of what she was, to commitment from him. She waited in tense silence but none of them were forthcoming.

After a long time, she sat up and reached for her clothes. As she put them on, she was conscious of an aching sadness inside her.

He watched her, his expression taut. 'What's the matter, Jill?'

'Nothing. The others will be back soon so I'm getting dressed.'

'You're also shutting me out. Why?'

'Am I? I thought you were the one doing that.'

He raised an ironic eyebrow. 'Just because I don't want to complicate what we share?'

'Accepting me as I am isn't complicating anything,' she almost shouted. 'But you can't, can you?'

'I don't know what you mean.'

'Oh no? Then how come you said I *was* a journalist, past tense?'

'Surely you don't mean to write your story now, after what happened between us?'

So she was right, his acceptance was conditional. All she had to do to retain his love was to abandon all that she was and did. How would he react if she laid down the same conditions? Maybe he had even made love to her with the express purpose of cajoling her to abandon the article. The possibility chilled her and she felt an urge to strike back. 'How do you know it wasn't research *for* the article?' she asked.

The colour drained from his face. 'My God, you

wouldn't stoop so low! Or would you? I don't suppose I'll find out until I read about it in the *Sydney Voice*.'

'You really don't think much of me, do you?' she said in a disappointed monotone. 'I won't write an exposé, if that's what you're worried about. All I mean to do is write the article we agreed upon. You owe me that. I played my part as agreed.'

'Is that what you were doing just now, playing a part?'

She couldn't let him think she was as manipulative as he was. 'No. I wanted it as much as you did.'

His hands tightened on the edge of the bedsheet. 'Then why does it have to end?'

Because it wasn't real, couldn't he see that? He was using her just as Terry had done. 'It's no good, I must write the story,' she said flatly. 'If I don't, I won't get the promotion I need to win Georgina back.'

His eyes flashed fire. 'Hang the promotion! I can give the two of you everything you need.'

Terry had said much the same when he proposed marriage, and look how it had ended up? She shook her head. 'It's not the same. I have to do it myself.'

He shook his leonine head in frustration. 'Why, Jill? Don't you trust me? You've come to mean more to me than I ever dreamed possible. I won't let you down.'

'Don't, please.' He probably meant it now, but she couldn't take the risk. Once he got his own way, it would be all over, like her marriage to Terry. For men like him and Midas, the thrill of the chase was what mattered.

A distant purring sound heralded the return of the

crew. They heard voices as the men came aboard, then the dinghy set out again to bring the others back from their shore excursion. She heard it all with a sense of detachment, as if she wasn't physically present at all.

She travelled back to Vincero in the same mood, taking no part in the lively discussion between Gerhardt and Robert Waya about the wonders of the Aboriginal cave paintings. Even Mr Yamamoto joined in with his limited English. Only Midas, his mood as black as hers, was aware of her withdrawal, but he made no attempt to involve her in the conversation or to participate himself. It was just as well that the others were too excited to notice.

Back at Vincero, she hurried to her room but was intercepted by Ted, his face grave as she almost cannoned into him. He reached out to steady her. 'Mrs Casey, I have an urgent message for you,' he informed her.

She blinked at him. 'A call? From who?'

'From Mr Casey. It's about your daughter.'

She tried to push past him. 'Is Terry on the phone? Let me speak to him.'

'We didn't know what time you'd be back so he left a message. Your little girl is ill and is asking for you. They suspect glandular fever.'

The room spun crazily for a moment then she regained control with an effort. 'When did he call?'

'Just a few minutes before you returned.'

She felt rather than heard Midas come up behind her. He must have heard everything. She gave him a beseeching look. Surely he wouldn't hold her to her word and keep her here when her child was ill and needed her?

The compassion in his dark gaze was her answer. He looked past her to Ted. 'Has Daniel left for Sydney yet?'

The security man shook his head. 'He had some maintenance work to do on the chopper but he's leaving at any minute.'

'Stop him, will you?' His searing gaze swept over Jill. 'Tell him he's got a passenger.'

CHAPTER SEVEN

PACKING took her very little time. Most of the clothes she'd worn on Vincero belonged to Midas's sister. Jill left them hanging in the dressing room. The metallic bikini was a poignant reminder that she and Midas had shared much more than a dressing-room. What on earth had possessed her to let him make love to her, knowing that he despised everything she stood for?

Her desire had been fuelled by the hope that things had changed between them. It wasn't all wishful thinking on her part. The electric sense of awareness which crackled into being whenever they were in the same room was definitely mutual. And she hadn't imagined her own galvanic responses when he kissed her. Nor the way his heartbeat quickened in return.

Just thinking about him made her feel light-headed. No, she wasn't imagining any of it. What *was* pure fantasy was the hope that he would change his attitude towards her work. His assumption that she would drop the story on him because they'd made love showed her how foolish her expectation was.

She sighed. Maybe the hope itself was unreasonable. If she had lost a partner and a child, wouldn't she hate the people responsible? Yes, she conceded, she would. She only hoped she would be wise enough to separate the guilty from the innocent in her mind.

Daniel had provided a small overnight bag with the

personal items she had ordered when she arrived. Now she packed the last of her things into it and zipped it shut. Soon she would be on her way back to Sydney and all this would be a memory. At the thought, a wave of desolation washed over her.

Midas appeared in the doorway and his dark eyes mirrored her distress. 'Don't worry, Jill. I'm sure your daughter will be all right.'

He thought she was sad only because of Georgina, she realised. What would he say if she told him that, in the midst of her concern for her daughter, she was also torn apart by the prospect of leaving him?

As if he read her mind, he said, 'Would you like me to fly back with you?'

The thought of having him at her side for a little longer was enough to set her heart leaping. It was all she could do not to tell him so. But her problems were none of his concern and she had no right to drag him into them. 'It's kind of you,' she said, 'but your guests need you here.'

He smothered what sounded like an oath. 'They're leaving later tonight anyway,' he said. 'If you need me. . .'

If? She had never needed anyone more than she needed him at that moment. She had no doubt that his offer was sincere, but if she accepted there would be strings attached. She would feel morally bound to abandon the story and the promotion which might help her win Georgina back. She couldn't risk it, not after her experience with Terry who had promised so much but delivered only heartache.

'Thank you, but I'll be fine,' she repeated. 'I feel guilty enough taking up Daniel's time as it is.'

There was a harsh glitter in Midas's eyes as if she had disappointed him in some way. Had he expected her to beg him to come with her? He shook his head as if to clear it. 'Don't worry about Daniel. He's paid to fly where and when I want him to. He had to take the chopper back to Sydney tonight in any case. We were just lucky that his repair work kept him here or he'd be gone by now.'

She picked up the small bag. 'Speaking of which, I'd better not detain him any longer.'

He took the case from her and their fingers brushed, electric awareness arcing between them. She jerked her hand away, earning a speculative look. But he made no comment and they made their way downstairs and out to where Daniel waited with the helicopter.

The rotor blades were already turning but Midas set her bag down and took her by the shoulders. 'I'm sorry you have to leave like this. I was hoping for a different outcome.'

A happy ever after in which he promised eternal love and she vowed not to write about him? She had stopped believing in fairy-tales long ago. She made herself shrug, determined not to let him see how difficult the parting was for her. 'It had to end some time. It's better if it's quick and painless.'

'Quick but never painless,' he denied. 'There's so much I still want to say to you.'

She squeezed his hand and the contact started bright tears in her eyes. She blinked hard. 'I think we said it all this afternoon, don't you?'

A muscle worked in his jaw. 'No, I don't. We both

said more than was probably prudent. I don't intend to let it rest there.'

Her hand was cupped around his and the warmth permeated her fingers. If she stayed another moment she would break down and tell him that she hadn't meant what she said. But that would mean examining the alternatives, which she wasn't ready to do yet. 'I have to go,' she insisted.

He fished in his pocket and held out a key. 'This belongs to my penthouse at the Sirius. If you need a place to stay, use it.'

Startled, she stared at the key but made no move to take it. 'I have my own place in Balmain.'

'But you don't know what will happen with Georgina. You may need to be near her at a hospital or something. My staff can help you with transportation or anything else you need. Please?'

Arguing would only delay her departure further so she thrust the key into her handbag. 'I probably won't need it, but thank you for the offer.' She turned towards the helicopter.

He caught her arm and spun her against him, winding her. 'Jill—call and let me know how your daughter is, no matter how late it gets. I won't relax until I know everything is all right.'

His embrace drove every sensible thought from her mind. She could only nod, achingly aware of every sculptured line of his hard, masculine body as he held her. 'I promise.'

'Thank you. God speed, now.' His mouth seared a path across her forehead and skimmed her parted lips. Then he turned her towards the helicopter and strode back to the house.

On the way to Vincero, she had savoured the luxury
of the corporate helicopter with its jet-aircraft-style
cabin and blissfully comfortable seats. Now she was
merely grateful for the quietness in the cabin which
enabled her to sort out her tangled thoughts.

Half of her was sick with worry about Georgina.
How ill was she? From the little Jill knew about
glandular fever, it was serious. Why hadn't she
thought to telephone Terry and find out the exact
situation before taking to the skies? She'd been too
distressed to think of it and now it was a struggle to
keep her errant imagination in check until she knew
just what was wrong.

The other half of her was still reeling from the
effects of Midas's kiss. It had been almost possessive,
as if he hated parting from her. If he really wanted to
see her again, was his attitude softening towards her
at last? And if so, where did they go from here?

By the time they approached Terry's property on
the outskirts of Parramatta, her head ached from
trying to make sense of it.

She had never expected to be grateful for the
helicopter pad which Terry had installed behind his
house. When news of his plans got out, it had caused
an upheaval among their neighbours. But he needed
helicopter access for the times when a major story
broke and he had to fly to the television station at
short notice. Privately she had thought his excuse
made him sound like a prima donna, but she had
defended him publicly, and now had cause to be
thankful as Daniel brought the helicopter down
towards the house.

Terry's house, Redruth, was set on a rise, with

acres of green lawn surrounding it. It had been built in colonial times as a country home for an officer in the New South Wales Rum Corps and retained its distinctive lime-washed exterior and bull-nosed veranda roof made of iron.

Jill remembered how impressed she had been with her first sight of the place. After her parents' suburban house it had seemed unbelievably grand. When Terry asked her to give up working to run Redruth, she had readily agreed.

Now she was returning to the house for the first time since the divorce, having entertained Georgina at her flat when it was her turn to look after their daughter.

The helicopter rotors had all but stopped spinning before she realised they'd landed. The cabin door opened and Daniel helped her out. Terry was waiting at the edge of the helipad, his expression envious as he studied the sleek lines of the helicopter.

'Welcome home, Jill. Quite a stylish arrival.'

'It's hardly home,' she commented, turning to the pilot. 'Daniel was kind enough to bring me here as quickly as possible.'

Having given him the opening, she waited for him to tell her more about Georgina's illness, but he seemed more interested in Daniel. 'Good to meet you,' he said, offering his hand. 'I'm Terry Casey.'

Since he possessed one of the best-known faces on television, Daniel must have known who he was the moment he set eyes on him. But the pilot merely smiled and returned the handshake. 'Daniel Prasad, personal pilot to Mr Midas Thorne.'

'So this is how the other half travels,' Terry

enthused. 'An Agusta is worth a bit, isn't it?' He walked around the helicopter, commenting on the retractable undercarriage until Daniel accepted his cue and gave him a tour of the craft.

Fuming with impatience, Jill stood it as long as she could. 'Enjoy your toy, I'm going to see my daughter,' she said and swung towards the house.

Georgina's bedroom was at the back, overlooking the garden. When Jill walked in, Kay Lloyd was playing a board game with the little girl. Seeing Jill, the governess jumped to her feet. 'Mrs Casey! I didn't expect you to get here so quickly.'

'I flew,' she said shortly. Kay must have heard the chopper arrive. 'How is she?'

The governess glanced at her young charge. 'She's fine.'

Georgina, who'd been absorbed in her game until then, finally looked up and saw the new arrival. 'Mummy! It is you,' she screamed in childish delight, bouncing up and down as she held out her arms.

Jill dropped on to the bed, hugging the child as if she would never let her go. Then she held her at arm's length. 'Let me look at you.' The tell-tale signs of fever were there in the too-bright eyes and flushed cheeks, but otherwise she looked surprisingly well. 'What did the doctor say?'

Georgina chewed her lower lip. 'He said I've got a walrus,' she said with a rush.

Jill's startled gaze flew to Kay Lloyd. 'A what?'

'A virus,' the governess supplied. 'She has to stay in bed for twenty-four hours but that's all.'

Jill felt weak with relief. 'Then it isn't glandular fever?'

Before the governess could answer, Terry appeared in the doorway. 'It was a possibility,' he said, 'but the doctor diagnosed a simple viral infection which will pass in a day or so.'

Anger brought the colour flooding into Jill's cheeks. 'I'd like to speak to you,' she said as evenly as she could, although her voice trembled with the effort. She smiled at the little girl. 'You go on playing your game with Kay while I talk to Daddy, all right?'

'OK. Are you going to talk about my walrus?'

'We most certainly are.'

Jill's smile lasted until they were out of earshot of the child's room, then her furious gaze raked her ex-husband. 'Why did you let me think it was glandular fever? I was worried sick all the way down here.'

He gave a non-committal shrug. 'It could have been.'

'But it wasn't,' she hissed back. 'Didn't you know how frantic I'd be when I got your message?' No wonder he hadn't wanted to speak to her directly.

Seeing his total lack of concern for her feelings, she felt a shock of discovery. Terry was a plastic person, a creation of the medium he represented. Beneath the polished exterior there was no substance, no compassion, just a shell waiting to be filled with whatever emotion was appropriate for the story currently going to air.

Even his widely quoted opinions were written for him and read off an autocue. Midas Thorne was ten times the man Terry was. He was real, solid and substantial. Someone worthy of her love, she realised with another jolt.

'Did it ever occur to you that I might want to see you?' Terry asked almost petulantly.

Her scepticism showed on her face. 'There's a first time for everything, I suppose.'

'It's true,' he insisted. 'I admit I used Georgina's illness as leverage, but she *was* asking for you. I didn't make that up.'

Another thought occurred to her. 'How did you know where to find me?'

'Your buddies at the *Voice* told me where you were. The hardest part was tracking down a phone number for Vincero. That took real ingenuity.'

Which Terry possessed in abundance. She wondered who at the newspaper had given her away. It was unlikely to be Bill Downey. He would want the story kept under wraps until it appeared. Then she had it. Jeff Pullen had been in Bill's office when she'd called to tell them her whereabouts. He and Terry had attended university together, another thing they had in common besides their lack of sensitivity.

Terry watched her work it out. 'Yes, it was Jeff,' he said in answer to her unspoken question. 'Don't hold it against him.'

She didn't, knowing how persuasive Terry could be when he wanted something. Her eyes narrowed with suspicion. 'I can't believe you went to all that trouble out of a desperate need to see me again.'

He had the grace to look uncomfortable. 'It was partly the reason. Once I knew you were with Midas Thorne, I wanted to know what was going on.'

'Was your interest personal or professional?' she couldn't resist asking.

'Both, dammit. You were my wife. I'm entitled to care what happens to you.'

If he did, it was another first, she thought sourly. 'It wouldn't be because I'm the only journalist Midas Thorne has allowed near him, would it?'

He shifted from one foot to the other, providing the unusual sight of an ill-at-ease Terry Casey. 'I admit I was curious, but I was also worried for your sake. Thorne isn't your type.'

His reasoning was all too transparent. Having cold-shouldered her since the divorce, his interest had been rekindled when he'd found out she was with Midas Thorne. 'You needn't worry about Midas and me,' she said heavily.

His eyebrows arched. 'So it's Midas now, is it? Are you two lovers?'

Her silence gave her away and his gaze hardened. 'You *are*. Is that the price you paid for your story?'

Her palm itched to connect with his handsome, unfeeling features. 'Of all the vicious, cruel——'

'Accurate?' he queried.

This time she did lash out and she stared in horrid fascination at the livid outline of her fingers on his cheek. 'Don't ever say that again.'

He seemed more amused than shocked and touched his face with a probing hand. 'My, my. The worm has turned, hasn't she? Of course, I know why you're doing this.'

She massaged her tingling fingers, sorry that she'd let him provoke her. He wasn't worth her anger. 'I don't know what you're talking about.'

'Don't you? I think you're using Thorne to make me jealous so I'll dance to your tune.'

Only Terry could think of something so outrageous. She shook her head blindly. 'You're wrong. You have nothing I want any more, Terry.'

'Not even Georgina?'

Her heart missed a beat. 'She has nothing to do with this.'

His long lashes hooded his eyes which were suddenly glittering and hard. 'She has everything to do with it. Give yourself to Thorne and you'll never get her back, I swear it.'

Her head came up as she fought to conceal her fear from him. 'Surely that's up to the courts to decide?'

'They decided in my favour once.'

'A decision I intend to challenge as soon as I have the means.'

His expression underwent a sea change from cold to stormy and for the first time, she saw a flicker of fear on his face. 'You aren't planning to marry Thorne, are you?'

'Hardly. I'm up for a big promotion and once I get it, I'll see you in court, I promise.'

The fear was replaced by mocking cynicism. 'And the Thorne profile is your passport to that promotion, isn't it?'

There was no point in dissembling. 'Yes, it is. As you pointed out already, it will be an exclusive.'

'You've come a long way, Jill.'

It was said with such sincerity that she froze, her retort choked back. Terry was actually *complimenting* her on her achievement. 'Then you accept that I didn't sleep my way into the assignment?' she asked.

'I'm sorry for implying it,' he startled her by

saying. 'I guess I've been worried about Georgina, too.'

'Apology accepted,' she said evenly but suspicion still clouded her mind. It wasn't like Terry to apologise for anything he said or did. Unless he had changed drastically since their divorce and she doubted it, somehow.

'You look suspicious,' he all but read her mind. 'Can't you allow for the fact that I miss you? When Georgie started asking for you, it seemed like the perfect excuse to get you here. I knew you wouldn't come for any other reason.'

She spread her hands in a gesture of confusion. 'Is it any wonder, when you've tried so hard to come between me and my child?'

'Our child,' he corrected her. 'All right, I admit I was bitter about splitting up. I never wanted the divorce, remember?'

Of course not. He had everything he wanted including a dutiful bride at home, a child, and all the women he wanted on the side. No wonder he found it ideal! 'It's too late for this,' she said tiredly. 'Just let me see Georgina and get out of here.'

His hand strayed to her arm and he began to stroke it absently, as if hardly aware of what he was doing. 'Don't rush away, Jill. Stay here tonight, in case Georgina wants you during the night.'

It was more likely to be Terry who wanted her during the night, she thought with a twinge of alarm. She couldn't risk staying under his roof. Yet she was torn by the possibility that her child might actually need her. 'I'll talk to Georgie first and see how she is,' she demurred. 'But I'll probably have Daniel take me back to the city afterwards.'

Terry's face darkened again. 'Thorne is being awfully generous towards you, given his reputation with journalists.'

'We're friends,' she said quietly, aware that the truce was over. Seeing that he wasn't going to get his own way, Terry was quickly reverting to type.

'Very well, have it your way,' he said cuttingly. 'Go talk to Georgina. I'll be outside, taking another look at that chopper.'

Feeling uneasy, she watched him go. Terry had never been unduly interested in mechanical things. He loved fast, luxurious cars, but for show rather than to drive or tinker about with. Helicopters were just another kind of fast transportation. Still, the Agusta was a stunning helicopter. Maybe his interest in it was genuine.

Dismissing her anxiety, she was smiling cheerfully by the time she returned to Georgina's room. The game was over and the little girl was colouring in with crayons. She grinned when she saw Jill. 'Guess what I'm colouring?'

Jill glanced at the thickly outlined figure, smudged over with purple crayon. 'I give up. What?'

'A walrus,' Georgina giggled. 'Kay says I have a vire. . .vire. . .'

'A virus,' Jill supplied. 'It's a kind of germ which makes you feel bad for a while. But it soon goes away.' Even since she arrived, the child's fever had diminished. She looked much more her normal self already. Jill curled up beside her on the bed and questioned Georgina gently about her life these days.

How was school? Was she coping with the angry
boys? The child's bubbly answers soon satisfied her
that all was well.

An hour flew past as Georgina begged Jill to sing
just one more song, or draw one more picture for her
to colour in. With the child cuddled in the crook of
her arm, Jill felt a glow of contentment. This was
what it would be like when the two of them were
together again for always.

'Do you know how I got here?' she asked
conspiratorially.

Georgina giggled. 'I know. You came in a helly-
clopter. Look, there it goes now.'

Jill followed Georgina's pointing finger. The helicopter was indeed rising above the treetops and the
whirrup of the rotors reached them through the glass.
Jill's anger rose. Why was Daniel leaving without her?

She slid her arm out from under Georgina. 'Excuse
me a minute, darling. I have to go and see Daddy.'

'Are you staying with us now?' the child asked
anxiously.

Fighting tears, Jill shook her head. 'Sorry, no. I've
explained why I can't live here any more but I'll come
back to see you first thing tomorrow, I promise.'

'It isn't the same.'

'I know, darling, but I can't help it. How about a
big smile for me? A walrus smile?'

At this, Georgina broke into a grin. 'Silly Mummy.
I told you I don't have a walrus.' She opened her
arms for a hug. Holding her tightly, Jill repeated her
promise to return next morning then hurried out of
the room before Georgina could see the tears welling
in her eyes.

Terry was in the living-room, a glass of scotch in his hand, when she stormed in. 'Why did you send Daniel away?'

'It seemed silly to keep him waiting around when you could have changed your mind about staying.' His voice turned the statement into a question.

'You know I wouldn't. Now you've cost me a fortune in cab fares back to the city.'

He took a sip of his drink. 'Stubborn as ever, aren't you? And so damned sure that you're right. I suppose you're heading back to that dog box in Balmain?'

He was referring to her flat. OK, it was small, but it wasn't as cramped as he made it sound. She was about to retort that it was her destination when an icy feeling gripped her. Why did it matter to Terry where she was going? Unless he had some crazy idea of following her to try and persuade her to come back to him?

She reached a rapid decision. 'Of course I'm going to my flat. Where else would I be going?' To Midas Thorne's penthouse, she had already decided, but she didn't want to say so. She rang for a taxi and gave Balmain as her destination. She would have to stop there to collect her things, so it wasn't a lie. But she would ask the cab to wait and take her to the Sirius afterwards.

Luckily a taxi had just dropped off a passenger in a nearby street and he arrived within minutes of her call. Without comment, Terry helped her into the car and handed her the overnight bag Daniel had left behind. 'I've told Georgina I'll see her tomorrow,' she said, watching his face.

His expression gave no clues as to his plans. 'Until

tomorrow, then. Sleep well. Dream of me.' Then he
closed the cab door and it drove off.

She sagged against the upholstery, feeling as if
she'd just run a marathon. Dream of him, indeed!
She was more than ever convinced that he intended
to surprise her by arriving at her Balmain flat tonight.
Well he would be the one getting the surprise, when
he found out she wasn't there.

The staff at the penthouse were expecting her, she
discovered when the taxi deposited her at the Sirius
Hotel. As soon as she gave her name, she was whisked
into the private elevator and up to the apartment
which occupied the top two floors of the building.

It was unbelievable, she thought, as she wandered
from room to room in wide-eyed amazement. The
luxury of the place was breathataking. Marble bathrooms with gold fittings and floral handbasins, a sauna
leading off the equally grand main bedroom with its
grey French velvet ceiling and coverings, repro-
duction Louis furnishings and cedar panelling.

Gold figurines were displayed on the coffee-table in
the living-room and the walls were covered with
paintings by famous artists. There was even a Pro
Hart in one of the bathrooms.

A city-based version of Mrs Kimber showed Jill to
a guest suite which would have been the master
bedroom in any other apartment. It possessed a full-
sized bathroom with sunken spa bath, and fabulous
views over the roof-tops of Sydney. By night, it was
like a scattering of diamonds on a black velvet cloth.

She accepted the housekeeper's offer of a 'light'
supper, which turned out to be a caviar omelette

followed by a Grand Marnier soufflé which would have done a restaurant proud.

She ate in solitary splendour at a hand-made Italian marble table which looked as if it could seat twelve. The only thing missing was Midas himself.

She pictured him seated opposite her at the long table. For some reason, she had a sudden fantasy of him spooning the black caviar into her mouth. The vision provoked such a flood of erotic feelings that she almost choked.

Her response was so strong that she could no longer ignore what she was feeling. She was in love with Midas Thorne. The realisation had been growing ever since they had made love aboard his boat. What happened hadn't been mere physical attraction, it had been her body's recognition of her soul's deepest needs.

She needed him, not as a man of power who could smooth her path through life, but as her kindred spirit and helpmate for better or for worse.

Terry must have guessed she was in love with Midas, even before she knew it herself. Seeing it must have made him all the keener to win her back; not because he wanted her himself, but because he couldn't bear to lose her to another man.

While she lived alone, Terry didn't care. Now, at the first sign of another man's interest, he was prepared to pursue her again.

She stifled a hysterical laugh. Terry needn't have worried. Just because she loved Midas, it didn't mean that her love was returned. In fact, it was the very opposite. To him she was the enemy. He might *make* love to her, but loving her was a very different matter.

CHAPTER EIGHT

'I'D like to speak to Mr Thorne, please. It's Jill Casey calling.'

'I'm sorry, Mrs Casey. Mr Thorne left on the launch with his business associates a couple of hours ago. Can I give him a message for you?'

She frowned at the telephone. Midas had asked her to let him know how Georgina was, no matter how late the hour. The decision to leave Vincero with his guests must have been a sudden one. 'Do you know when he'll be back, Ted?' she asked the security man.

'I'm afraid not.'

'Well, when he does, would you tell him my daughter's much better?' she said. 'He asked me to let him know.'

'I'll tell him. Goodnight, Mrs Casey.'

Slowly she replaced the receiver and curled her feet under her on the leather-upholstered couch. Where had Midas gone at such short notice? Her glance flickered to the front door of the penthouse, as if she expected him to walk in at any moment. Which was silly. He didn't even know she was staying here, although he had given her the key in case she wanted to. Obviously, he hadn't intended to be here at the same time.

It was late and she should probably go to bed but, with the staff gone for the evening, the penthouse seemed huge and lonely. Unlike at Vincero, the housekeeper, the maid and the valet only slept here when they were needed. Otherwise they lived in the staff quarters of the hotel itself. When Midas was in residence, they took turns being on call in case they were needed.

Restlessly, she prowled around the apartment. There were several more bedrooms, each with its own en-suite bathroom as luxuriously appointed as the one off her room. There was a spacious kitchen equipped with every modern appliance. Midas must entertain a lot when he was in town. Trying out the furniture, Jill felt like Goldilocks, exploring the three bears' cottage. Except that this was no cottage and the 'bear' was more likely to be found in the stock exchange than the forest.

The master bedroom took up most of the second level. One wall was lined with cedar bookshelves which were crammed with books, most of them read, judging by their well-thumbed appearance. The other wall was lined with wardrobes, the door panelled with mirrors. The en-suite bathroom was also panelled with mirrors and the bed stood on a platform in the centre of the room.

The bed was large and inviting and she had a sudden startling vision of Midas lying there, the sheets pulled taut over his muscular chest. In the vision, his arms opened to her and desire curled inside her like a living thing. Tears blurred her eyes and she turned hastily away.

Feeling like an interloper in his private domain, she was about to close the door when a leather-bound photo album lying on a bedside table caught her eye. Mechanically, she moved to it and opened the cover, suppressing a shiver when she saw that it had belonged to Yolande Thorne. Her feminine signature was scrawled on the flyleaf.

Curiosity got the better of her. She sat down on the bed, pulled the album on to her lap and began to leaf through the pages.

Many of the pictures were of a pretty young woman with clear grey eyes and sun-streaked blonde hair. Yolande, Jill concluded. The baby in her arms must have been Michael Junior, Midas's son. They looked so vibrantly alive that it was hard to believe they were both gone. Yolande's zest for living fairly shone out of the pages of the album.

Jill studied her in fascination, seeking some clue as to why Midas had loved her with such passion that he still blamed a whole profession for causing her death five years before. Only a powerful love could have kindled such a durable hatred. Looking at the pictures, Jill couldn't believe that Yolande would have wanted Midas to grieve for so long. She looked incapable of hating anyone, so lustrous and clear was her gaze and so infectious her smile. Jill found herself smiling in response.

Turning the pages, she came to an earlier photo and a stab of something very like jealousy pierced her. It was of Yolande and Midas together, both very young and making such a handsome pair that it hurt to look at them, knowing their love was doomed.

The photo was loose and Jill turned it over. On the back was written, 'Kalgoorlie, 1975'. Was the mining town where they met? If so, it explained Yolande's fresh, unspoiled country-girl looks. And also why she was affected by the pressure of Midas's high-powered existence. In a mining environment, Midas's raw masculinity would have a powerful appeal. Ambitious though he might have been then, neither of them could have foreseen the heights he would scale in just a few short years. Could it have contributed to the breakdown which led to Yolande's death?

There were many more photos and Midas looked more handsome and confident in each one, as his personal growth matched his success. Some were taken at Vincero, Jill recognised with a jolt. Others showed travel scenes from different parts of the world. In all of them, Yolande was in the background, usually behind Midas, as if she was symbolically withdrawing from his hectic lifestyle.

Jill's heart went out to the dead woman. As Terry Casey's wife she had also been caught in a whirlwind existence, sometimes feeling as if she was going mad. It was only the fact of having two journalists for parents which had saved Jill, accustoming her to the hurly-burly of the news world from childhood. As a teenager she had been tugged back and forth between her divorced parents, so she was used to having more than one home base. It didn't mean she enjoyed it, but she was better equipped to cope than Yolande would have been.

The baby, Michael, looked enchanting, and Jill's womb contracted in protest when she thought of his short life being so cruelly ended. There was no doubt whose son he was. He possessed none of Yolande's golden features. His eyes were as dark as his father's and his wisps of hair were already coal-black.

Jill's eyes misted as she closed the album and put it carefully back on to the nightstand. Midas had lost almost more than a man could be expected to bear. After seeing the photos Jill wasn't sure the media were wholly to blame for Yolande's breakdown, but she understood Midas's need to blame someone or something. No wonder he hated the Press so vehemently. How he must regret making love to her on his boat. Had he left Vincero so abruptly to avoid her call, knowing he had betrayed his principles?

For her, it was different. Terry had all but convinced her she was frigid, so Midas's lovemaking came as a revelation. He had shown her how wonderful it could be, and her heart ached to think there was no future in it, as long as he clung to his prejudices.

Cold suddenly, although the air-conditioned apartment was warm, she flung herself out of his bedroom and down to her own room. Perhaps a hot bath would settle her sufficiently for sleep.

The sunken spa bath filled surprisingly quickly and was soon bubbling invitingly. It was just the balm she needed after her unsettling day. Eagerly, she shed her clothes and stepped into the water, reaching for the switch which triggered a bank of massaging jets of water.

Resting against the contoured bath while the jets massaged her muscles, she closed her eyes and tried to relax. It was difficult because her tired brain kept conjuring up images of Midas. Knowing that she loved him, she longed to be with him and have him hold her the way he had on his boat. She was becoming addicted to him, she realised. Yet to him she was no more than a passing fling. Even if she had agreed not to write the story, there was no guarantee that he would change. His wounds went deep. Her love, powerful though it was, might not be enough to heal them.

'Hello, Jill.'

Her eyes flew open and she looked up, for a split second wondering if she had conjured Midas up out of her own yearnings. But he was as large as life, and definitely real as he hunkered down beside the spa. Irrationally, she was glad that the foaming water hid her from his gaze.

'What are you doing here?' she asked.

'I could say the same to you.'

Anxiety gripped her. Had she presumed too much by coming here? 'You did say I could use the penthouse,' she reminded him.

'And I meant it, but you were so adamant that there was no need that I didn't expect to find you here.'

His nearness provoked a shiver, in spite of the warmth of the water. 'I didn't want Terry to know where I was, so I told him I was going to Balmain, then I gave the cab driver this address.'

'I see. Why didn't you want your husband to know where you were?'

'My ex-husband,' she corrected automatically. 'It's silly, but I thought he might follow me home. He. . .he wants me to come back to him.' She didn't add that Midas himself was the reason for Terry's renewed interest in her.

Thankfully, Midas didn't pursue the subject. 'And your daughter? How is she?'

'It's not as serious as I was led to believe. She has a virus but it's only a twenty-four-hour thing, not glandular fever at all.'

'He knows you very well,' Midas observed. 'He knew you'd come running if he made it sound serious enough. Why, I wonder?'

She burst a bubble with a flutter of her hand. 'I told you, to try to persuade me to come back.'

Lines of deep thought grooved Midas's forehead. 'Was that the only reason?'

She regarded him uncertainly. 'What else could there be?'

He stood up and reached for his tie. 'I don't know and I don't intend to waste any more time worrying about it.'

Tension radiated through her. 'What are you doing?'

'Joining you in there. It was designed for two, after all.'

The shock of his announcement set her senses spinning. She couldn't be as casual about his suggestion as he was. She had no defences left where he was concerned. 'I don't think it's a good idea,' she parried.

He shed his shirt and reached for his belt buckle. 'Why not? You look wonderfully relaxed.'

If she did, it was a triumph of acting skill, because every nerve-ending had quivered to life and her skin felt electrically charged at the prospect of sharing the spa bath with him. Large enough for two it might be, but there was no way to avoid touching each other and, in her present sensitised state, who knew where it would lead?

Before she could frame a convincing objection, he shed the last of his clothes and stepped into the steaming water. The bubbles rose up his magnificent body as he slid deeper into the water, then he settled on the seat opposite her, stretching out his long legs in front of him with a sigh of contentment. 'This is just what I needed.'

But not what she needed, she thought with a flaring of panic. Letting him make love to her had been a mistake and she was not about to repeat it. Sex for its own sake was for the likes of Terry Casey, who used people then discarded them without a backward glance. For her, it meant a sharing of minds and souls, not just bodies. Knowing that Midas couldn't love her, she couldn't give herself to him again and live with herself afterwards. Once was hard enough to bear.

Nevertheless, when his leg grazed hers, she was powerless to prevent the spasms of response which throbbed through her. It was as if someone had turned up the heat in the spa. Her skin burned and beads of perspiration stood out on her forehead, even though she'd been perfectly comfortable with the temperature only moments before. Her throat felt dry and she swallowed hard.

'Not too hot for you? I can turn it down,' Midas offered, his warm gaze surveying her flushed features.

'No, I. . .it isn't the heat.' For someone who made her living with words, it was suddenly awfully hard to string two of them together coherently.

He leaned towards her, stroking her forehead with the back of his hand. 'What's the matter, Jill?'

He didn't know. Even now, he still had no idea that she was in love with him. She didn't know whether to feel elated or cheated that he thought she took sex as lightly as he appeared to do. Surely he must know that she wouldn't have given herself to him unless she really cared about him?

'I think I've had enough,' she said, standing up and reaching for her towel. 'I'll leave you to your spa.'

His eyes darkened. 'Now I've spoiled it for you. Perhaps I should be the one to leave.'

She climbed out of the water and wrapped the bath sheet around herself. 'No, finish your spa. I'll get dressed and make us some coffee.'

It was said on the spur of the moment as an excuse to get away from his disturbing presence. But when she was dressed in a sea-green velvet house gown, with her damp hair caught in a tortoiseshell band, she regretted her impulsive offer. Sharing coffee would only prolong the encounter. She should have let him leave when he'd wanted to.

Why hadn't she? The question bothered her as she went through the motions of filling the coffee machine and fitting a filter paper into it. It was surprising how quickly she had begun to feel at home in the strange kitchen, finding things almost instinctively; like the coffee grounds, which were in the first cupboard she opened. It was almost as if she belonged here.

'Finding everything you need?'

Midas strolled into the kitchen. On cue, her heart began to hammer against her ribs. His skin was ruddy from the hot spa and his glossy black hair was moulded to his head like a gladiator's helmet. He was naked to the waist and dewdrops of water clung to his chest hair.

She watched, mesmerised, as a single drop of water, like a tear, rolled down his chest, dissipating against the waistband of his boxer shorts. She licked her lips tensely and tore her eyes away, fixing them on the coffee machine. 'I hope I've got this thing operating properly,' she said to disguise her confusion.

He moved closer. 'Let me help.'

His nearness set up a fresh clamour inside her. She fiddled with the machine, adjusting knobs which didn't need her attention. 'I can manage, thanks.'

His breath whispered against her neck. 'What's the matter? Don't I look the domestic type?'

She took refuge in a retort. 'How would I know whether you're domesticated when you're always surrounded by attentive staff?'

'But not this time.'

His statement reminded her shockingly that they were alone in this vast apartment. Even on the cruiser, she'd had the assurance that the crew could return at any time. Here, they had the place to themselves until morning. The hiss of the percolator was a welcome diversion.

'The coffee's ready,' she said, hoping he hadn't seen the colour which flooded her face at the thought.

'The coffee can wait.' Two long strides brought him across the kitchen to her side. His hands clasped her shoulders, his grip possessive as he turned her to face him. 'Jill, we have to talk.'

Talking was the last thing on her mind as her senses reeled in instant reaction to his touch. More than anything, she wanted to melt against the hard wall of his chest, rest her cheek in the crook of his shoulder and give herself up to the heady delight of loving him.

But how could she live with herself? If all they shared was sexual gratification, she was no better than Terry in her own mind. He was a user of people. Worse, he was proud of it. People were there to be used, he said. Do unto others before they do unto you. It wasn't how she wanted to live her life.

Unless and until Midas loved her, she would never share his bed again.

He sensed the change in her and held her at arm's length, his expression quizzical. 'What's the matter? You can't pretend I don't turn you on because I know the truth.'

'Yes, you do.' There was no point in denying what he had discovered for himself aboard the *Lady Why*.

'Then what is it?'

She was not, repeat not, going to beg for his love. If he couldn't set aside his prejudices and give it freely, then she would have to live without it. The prospect was painfully bleak but she made herself face it. 'Nothing's the matter, I'm just tired,' she dissembled.

His hands slid down her body and dropped to his sides. 'Perhaps you're right. It's been a long day for both of us, but especially for you. I should have realised that worrying about your daughter must have exhausted you.'

His glib explanation satisfied only himself but she let it pass. All she wanted was to be left alone. Here, beside him, she could hardly think straight and it was getting increasingly difficult to stick to her resolution. 'Do you mind if I pass on the coffee?' she asked, sounding more tired than she actually was. 'I'd like to go to bed.'

His searching gaze told her she could have put that a better way, but he let it pass. 'I think we could both use some sleep,' he agreed. 'I'll arrange a suite in the hotel for myself.'

'But what about your room here?'

'Not a good idea, as you've just reminded us both.'

So he had finally remembered why he couldn't love her, she thought with a sinking sensation. It had taken him long enough. It was irrational but she felt disappointed that he wasn't sleeping in the penthouse. It would have been some consolation, knowing he was sleeping nearby, although this way she would probably get more rest.

She turned aside. 'Then I'll say goodnight.'

'Goodnight Jill.' As she walked past, he caught her chin and pressed his mouth to hers. The kiss was no more than a fleeting feather-touch but it seared her like a brand. She had to steel herself not to look back, lest he see the havoc the slight contact had wrought.

But he stopped her again at the kitchen door. 'I still mean to have that talk, Jill. Will you have lunch with me tomorrow? I have business meetings all morning or I'd make it breakfast.'

By the time she looked at him, she had regained her composure sufficiently to say, 'I promised Georgina I would spend the morning with her. I can't be back by lunchtime if I want to spend any time with her.'

'How about dinner, then?'

What could they possibly say to each other which would change anything? Was he going to offer her a permanent position as his mistress? She had filled the role admirably during the last week. But there was a

difference between posing as his mistress and actually
taking on the role, knowing he didn't love her.

All the same, she couldn't bring herself to rebuff
him completely. 'I don't know,' she hedged.

'I could convince you,' he said, the caressing note
in his voice leaving her in no doubt of how he would
manage such a task. Her breath caught in her throat.

'Very well, dinner then,' she heard herself whisper.
Her traitorous heart lifted at the prospect. She was
only prolonging her own suffering by agreeing. As
soon as her story appeared in the *Sydney Voice*, he
would be forcibly reminded of the gulf between them.
But the dinner was tomorrow night. Why not enjoy
his company while she still could?

Before she abandoned all her scruples and begged
him to spend the night in the penthouse, she fled to
her own room where she lay awake, tense and
unhappy, until she heard the front door close behind
him. Only then did she relax enough to fall asleep.

Although she went to bed later than usual, she
awoke at her usual time of seven-thirty and took in
her surroundings in bewilderment. Where was she?
Then she remembered. She was at Midas's penthouse. She was going to spend the whole morning
with her daughter. Tonight, she could look forward
to an evening in Midas's company. What more could
she ask from a day?

The discovery lifted her spirits as she showered and
breakfasted, enjoying the luxury of having her food
prepared and served by the housekeeper. It was
amazing how wonderful scrambled eggs could taste
when someone else did the cooking and washing up!

By the time she caught a taxi to her Balmain flat

and collected her car, it was later than she liked. She felt guilty succumbing to so much pampering and had to force herself to keep to the speed limit as she drove along the expressway to the outskirts of Sydney.

When she reached Redruth, Terry was nowhere in sight. Jill heaved a sigh of relief as Kay Lloyd let her in. She wasn't in the mood for verbal fencing with Terry today. Knowing how she felt about Midas, she wondered how she could ever have believed herself in love with someone as vain and shallow as Terry Casey.

'What did the doctor say?' she asked Kay as the governess led the way to Georgina's room.

'He's put her on antibiotics but says she can get up today if she wants to. Her fever's gone. You'd never guess she was ill.'

Jill laughed. 'I suppose she can't wait to get up?'

The governess nodded. 'I told her she could as soon as you arrived.'

Jill glanced around uneasily. 'Has Mr Casey left for work already?' Her tone said she hoped he had.

The governess's steps faltered. 'Actually, he's working at home this morning. One of his assistants came over and the two of them are working in the summerhouse.'

'A woman?'

The governess seemed reluctant to answer but Jill's silence gave her no option. 'Jennifer Golding. Do you know her?'

Mechanically, Jill nodded. She knew the woman. Long silky blonde hair, anorexic teenage figure, small high breasts. Just Terry's type. An icy despair overtook her. Terry would never change. But how he could amuse himself with his latest *assistant* when his daughter was ill and needed him? Her despair turned to anger but she masked it with an effort. 'I'd like to see Georgie by myself first.'

'Of course, Mrs Casey. I'll make myself some coffee. Would you like a cup?'

'Thank you. And I don't answer to Mrs Casey any more. Jill will do.'

With the statement, the last of her ties to Terry dropped away, leaving only the inescapable one of their daughter. But somehow, some way, she would get Georgina back. It was more vital than ever now. Thank goodness she hadn't let Midas talk her out of writing the story.

Georgina, looking adorable in a Laura Ashley nightdress, was building a tower out of Lego bricks on the floor when Jill entered. Her face lit up. 'Mummy! You did come!'

Jill swept the child into her arms. 'I promised, didn't I? Have I ever broken a promise to you?'

The child thrust out her lower lip. 'No, but you weren't here last night. I woke up and called and called for you.'

Dismay gripped Jill. How could she possibly explain the situation between her and Terry to a six-year-old? 'I told you I couldn't sleep here any more. But I said I'd come back first thing in the morning and here I am.'

'It isn't the same.' With a child's swift change of subject, she brightened. 'Mummy, what's a portant thing?'

Jill slid to the floor and clasped her hands around her bent knees. 'I don't know, darling. How was it used?'

'When you didn't come, Daddy said you had more portant things to do than run after me.'

The icy feeling returned. It had started already, Terry's campaign to turn Georgina against her. 'The word is "important",' she corrected. 'And Daddy's wrong. I didn't have anything more important to do. I spent the whole night worrying about you and wondering how you were.'

Apparently satisfied, Georgina nodded. 'Oh, that's all right, then. Will you help me build a Lego house now?'

The crisis had passed but its implications still tormented Jill. She had to make an effort to push her worries aside. Building the house helped. When it was finished, Georgina happily allocated bedrooms to each person she knew. Her father, Kay and several school friends were given rooms but Georgina frowned when she came to her mother. 'You don't sleep here. Do you still need a room in my house?'

Tears gathered in Jill's eyes. 'Pretend the house is your heart, darling. I'll always need a room in that.'

'OK, then you can have this one.' Georgina pointed to a corner room on the second floor of the multi-coloured building. 'There's one over.'

'Who's going to sleep there?' Jill asked.

The small face screwed up in concentration. 'Daddy's friend,' she said at last.

A feeling of dread assailed Jill. 'Which friend, sweetheart?'

'The ladies who come here with him. I can't say which one 'cause they change,' Georgina explained.

It was too much! What kind of upbringing was Georgina getting if she already knew that Daddy had lots of lady friends and 'they changed'? This had to be stopped and the sooner the better. Kay Lloyd came in with their coffee and Jill stood up. 'Can you mind Georgina for a few minutes? I must see Terry.'

The governess looked flustered. 'It's not a good idea. They're very busy right now. I tried to offer them coffee and nearly got my head bitten off.'

The metaphor made Georgina giggle, but Jill was in no laughing mood. 'I don't care how busy they are. It's time Terry found out the meaning of responsibility.'

Where she found the courage to storm out past the pool, and thunder on the summerhouse door, she didn't know. Terry had always been able to intimidate her before. This time, however, he'd gone too far. Entertaining his lady friends at the expense of his daughter was intolerable. She heard a muffled response from inside. 'Get lost, Kay!'

'It isn't Kay. It's me, Jill.'

'Good lord, I forgot she was coming.' Terry's voice carried clearly through the wooden door and Jill smiled grimly as scrambling noises came from inside.

Moments later, Terry opened the door a crack. His clothes were dishevelled and he looked dazed. The pupils of his eyes were unusually large. 'What's a-matter?' he mumbled.

Over his shoulder, Jill saw his 'assistant' clutching her clothes around her. It was obvious what had been going on. But it wasn't their activities which shocked her to her core, so much as the acrid smell and the smoke which filled the room. She had never smoked pot in her life, but she'd shared a flat with people who did. There was no mistaking the smell.

'It's all right, Terry,' she said with deadly calm. 'I just wanted to tell you I was leaving.'

He looked startled. ''s that all? OK, g'bye then.'

The door was slammed in her face and a woman's giggles reached her through it. She thought she heard the words, 'stupid bitch' but she wasn't sure. It didn't matter anyway. She knew exactly what she had to do.

No matter what the court said, there was no way she could leave an impressionable six-year-old in the company of a man who behaved as irresponsibly as Terry. If she went to jail for it, she would protect her child from his debauched behaviour.

Kay Lloyd looked apprehensive when Jill strode back inside. 'Is everything all right?' She glanced over Jill's shoulder as if expecting a furious Terry to charge in after her.

'Everything's fine,' Jill said calmly. 'I wanted to check with Terry before I took Georgina out for the day.'

'Out? But——'

'Exactly.' Jill cut her short. 'I'll dress her while you put a change of clothes and her medication into a bag for me. I'll pick out some of her favourite toys and we'll be on our way.'

On their way where? Jill thought frantically as the governess did her bidding. She couldn't take Georgina home. When he came to his senses, it was the first place Terry would look.

There was only one solution. She still had the key to the penthouse. They could go there. Midas would know what to do.

CHAPTER NINE

THIS time there was no need to identify herself. As soon as Jill arrived at the Sirius Hotel, she was recognised and escorted to the private elevator where she and Georgina were whisked up to the penthouse level.

The lift driver smiled indulgently at the excited little girl. 'Do you like riding in elevators?'

'It scrunches my knees up,' she said, adding, 'but it's nearly as good as the zoo.'

Jill and the driver exchanged smiles. It was only when she reached the sanctuary of the apartment that the enormity of what she had done came crashing in on her. Her knees went weak.

As a journalist she had written about parents who kidnapped their own children without understanding the desperation which drove them to it. It had carried her along on a tidal wave, blinding her to everything but the need to protect her child.

From the moment she realised that Terry and his girlfriend had been smoking marijuana, she hadn't stopped to think. Putting Georgina in her car and bringing her to the Sirius were instinctive responses to her deepest mothering urges. She could no more fight them than she could fly.

Sensing her mother's distress, Georgina slipped a hand into Jill's. 'I like this place. It's pretty.'

Through her doubts and fears, Jill managed to nod

and smile. 'Yes, it is. It belongs to a friend of mine
who said we could stay here.'

It was an exaggeration, since Midas had never
included Georgina in his invitation. But when he
knew her predicament, she was sure he wouldn't
mind. He might know someone in the judicial system
who could advise her on what to do next. Some
parents simply vanished with their child, but she
couldn't imagine spending years in hiding. It was no
life for her or Georgina. The alternative, that she
might be forced to surrender the child to Terry, she
refused to think about.

Jill had been apprehensive about thrusting a child
on to Midas's staff but she needn't have worried.
According to the housekeeper, Midas's sister and her
children were regular visitors from Tasmania, and a
supply of toys and amusements was kept for them.
They were soon located and Georgina eagerly delved
into the box. Her cries reminded Jill of Christmas
morning, as each new novelty was unearthed.

'Look, a Barbie doll,' Georgina said. 'And look,
Mummy, she has tons and tons of clothes.'

'They're lovely, darling,' Jill agreed absently. She
was too preoccupied with her problems to give the
doll much attention. Her smile satisfied Georgina,
who settled down to dress the doll.

Jill was thankful for the respite. After paying for a
taxi back to the city from Parramatta yesterday, her
cash was running low. A pay-day had come and gone
while she was at Vincero, so she wasn't sure how
much money was left in her bank account. She would
need funds for herself and Georgina, and a retainer
for a lawyer to clarify their future. Midas would lend

her some money if she asked, but she balked at asking him, not wanting him to think she was taking advantage of his friendship.

Georgina thrust a dressed doll in front of Jill's face and she oohed and aahed obligingly. Then she excused herself to make a telephone call.

'Are you going to ring up Daddy?' Georgina asked.

He was the last person she would call. 'No, darling, just my boss, to see how he's managing without me.'

Bill Downey answered straight away. 'How's the star reporter?' he asked when she identified herself.

Weariness washed over her. He thought she was about to announce the success of her assignment. In truth, she hadn't given the profile a thought since completing the first draft at Vincero. The notes lay untouched at the bottom of her overnight bag. 'Your star reporter's going broke,' she said, injecting a cheerful note into her voice. 'Do you know if my last pay cheque was credited to my account?'

'What do you think?' he said, sounding surprised that she needed to ask. 'There's a sizeable bonus, besides.'

What on earth did he mean? 'A bonus? Isn't it a bit premature?'

'Hardly. Your husband delivered your copy last night. I held the Press so it made today's edition. It's dynamite stuff. The publisher's over the moon about it.'

Her husband had delivered her copy? 'Terry came to see you?' she echoed, hearing her voice coming from a long way away.

'That's right. He said your kid was sick and you couldn't leave her to deliver it yourself. Frankly, it can come by camel train as long as it's as good as this.'

What was he talking about? She hadn't written any article and she definitely hadn't asked Terry to deliver it for her. Her head felt as if it was packed with cotton wool and thinking was a struggle. 'He's my ex-husband,' she said stupidly, grasping the one fact which made sense.

The editor chuckled. 'Really? I got the impression that the two of you were back together. Your husband's quite a guy, isn't he?'

Unable to cope with much more, she agreed that Terry was indeed 'quite a guy', and hung up. Moments later she was scrabbling through her overnight bag, tossing clothes on to the bed and finally dumping the bag upside down before accepting that her precious notes were gone. Terry must have removed them when he'd taken the bag from Daniel Prasad. When the bag was given to her, she hadn't thought to check that the contents were intact.

But to write the story and hand it in as her work? She could hardly believe Terry would do such a thing. She had to see the article.

The housekeeper agreed to look after Georgina, offering to give her some lunch, while Jill went out to track down a copy of the *Sydney Voice*. The hotel could send it up, the woman suggested, but Jill was too agitated to wait a moment longer than necessary to see the article.

There was a newspaper shop in the hotel lobby and she waited only until she was outside the door to open the paper. When she came to the article, she gagged, feeling as if she was going to be ill there and then.

The profile took up two pages and was accompanied by several file photographs of Midas and an aerial shot of Vincero.

It was a two-column sidebar which caused her the greatest anguish. It described, in detail, the diamond coating process which Midas had explained to her in confidence. It was all there, from the way the process used plasma physics to excite a carbon-hydrogen gas to produce diamonds, to the practical applications and Midas's plans for the process in the drilling industry.

The pages shook in her fingers. None of this came from her notes. How had Terry learned about the top-secret process? Had he bribed one of Midas's partners? It seemed unlikely since they were the ones who had placed an embargo on any publicity. But how else could Terry have found out so much?

'Impressive, isn't it?'

Whirling around, she found Terry looking over her shoulder. Smooth-shaven and impeccably dressed, it was hard to reconcile his appearance now with the bleary-eyed creature she'd surprised in the summer-house this morning, stoned half out of his mind. 'What are you doing here?' she hissed.

'Following your trail,' he said equably. 'It wasn't hard to figure out where you would go.' His gaze flickered to the article open in her hands. 'Like your handiwork?'

'It isn't mine and you know it. I didn't write this stuff.'

'But Midas Thorne won't know that, will he?'

A deadly sense of calm replaced her trembling. Suddenly she understood what was going on. Terry knew that Midas didn't want any publicity for his process until he was ready, so he had placed the article over her byline knowing it would destroy any relationship between them. Terry couldn't have chosen a more effective way to come between her and Midas.

Her heart felt like a stone, cold and hard in her chest. Flesh and blood she might be on the outside, but inside she was as cold as the marble statues decorating the hotel lobby. Terry had killed her with his wanton act. Midas would never believe she hadn't betrayed him. His contempt for her would know no bounds. 'I'm going to demand that the paper prints a retraction,' she said, but recognised it as bravado. Bill would never agree, even if he accepted her version of what happened.

Terry gave her a sly smile. 'We both know you're wasting your time.' He took her arm in a possessive grip. 'Let's have a cup of coffee and talk about this.'

'We have nothing to talk about,' she spat out through clenched teeth.

He lowered his head so his mouth was level with her ear. 'How about a kidnapping?' he murmured. To an onlooker, he could have been murmuring endearments to her.

Her chalk-white face gave the lie to such a notion. She tried to wrench her arm free but his grip tightened. There was no way to escape without attracting attention and she didn't want to do that, with Georgina only a few floors above them. If provoked, Terry could well call the police and have them forcibly return Georgina to him. He would be within his rights.

She made herself relax. 'Very well, I'll come with you, but I can't stay long.'

'Is your lover waiting upstairs?' he asked nastily.

'It's none of your business.'

'But Georgina *is* my business and I mean to get her back, preferably with you, but without you if you insist on making things difficult.'

Her blood froze but no good would come of antagonising him, so she bit back a retort and allowed him to steer her to the coffee shop on the other side of the lobby. Designed like a sidewalk café, it had wrought-iron tables and chairs under gaily coloured umbrellas.

Terry chose a corner table and pulled out a chair for her. Numbly, she sat down, hardly hearing him order coffee for them both. Her mind could only grasp the fact that Terry had destroyed her. By making it appear as if she had betrayed Midas, he had effectively laid waste her future. There was no way she and Midas could work things out now.

Some masochistic streak made her ask, 'How did you do it?'

'Write the story, you mean? Your notes made it easy. I just tidied them up and produced a clean draft. I write a lot of my own news copy, you know?'

It was a reminder that he wasn't the 'talking head' many people dismissed him as. She refused to be sidetracked. 'I didn't mean the profile. I meant the sidebar, about the diamond coating process. It wasn't in my notes.' Knowing Midas didn't want it publicised until he was ready, she hadn't included that part of the briefing in her draft. It was only on tape and the tape was still at Vincero, where she'd left it.

A dangerous glitter lit up Terry's eyes. 'You should know better than to ask a journalist to reveal his sources. Besides, you could have talked in your sleep.'

'To do that, we'd have to sleep in the same room and we'll never do that as long as I live,' she vowed. 'Jeff Pullen was in on it, wasn't he?'

His hooded gaze gave her the answer she needed. 'He wrote the article for you, didn't he?'

'Give me some credit. I can string two words together, you know.'

Attacking his ego was getting her nowhere. Besides, what did it matter how he came by the story? As long as Midas believed she was responsible, the truth made little difference. Her slumped shoulders reflected her despair and she stirred her coffee mindlessly, the whirling liquid reflecting her kaleidoscopic thoughts.

Terry sugared his coffee liberally and added cream. Evidently he wasn't worried about putting on weight, although Jill thought that his lifestyle was staring to show in his thickening jowls and waistline. Dragging her eyes to his face, she asked wearily, 'What do you want from me?'

His gaze locked with hers. 'I told you, my daughter. Kidnapping is a criminal offence, even if you are her mother, so you may as well tell me where she is before matters get any worse.'

How could they possibly get any worse? 'I can't tell you where she is, but she's safe. Safer than with you and that pot-smoking creature you were entertaining this morning. How long do you think you'd retain custody of a child once the court heard about that?'

'You'd have to prove it, first.'

Her gaze was equally level. 'I could have Jennifer Golding called as a witness.'

His eyes narrowed. 'She wouldn't say anything to incriminate me. Her job and future depend on my goodwill.'

It was always the same story. 'What are you? Some kind of Svengali who bewitches these girls to get them to do your bidding?'

'Hardly. They're willing enough. Even you were, once.'

Mortified, she averted her eyes, knowing that once, she had been as vulnerable to Terry's charm as any of the others. 'I was a child,' she said in her own defence. 'I'll never be so stupidly innocent again.'

With a teaspoon, he drew patterns on the table-top. 'Do you know, you're my only failure?' He lifted his head and his eyes drilled into her, alight with a fanatical gleam which terrified her. 'I mean to have you back, Jill.'

'What's the point when I'm in love with another man?'

'You really think he'll feel the same after he reads today's *Voice*?'

Her downcast gaze told its own story. He knew as well as she did how Midas would react. Her chin lifted with a last attempt at defiance. 'Whether he does or not, you must be mad to think I'd come back to you after this.'

'Soon you'll have no choice. Give up, Jill. I can deal with any man who so much as looks at you. Haven't I proved it today?' He leaned forward. 'Make it easy on yourself and come back to me. You can have Georgina and give up this hand-to-mouth existence.'

'I'd rather starve.'

'You may have to. Thorne won't want you around after he reads the article. And the moment you appear outside with my daughter, I'll be waiting, with the law on my side.'

'Midas isn't as shallow as you seem to think.'

Terry gave an all-knowing smile which struck fear into her heart. 'Maybe not. But from what I'm told, he may not be around to worry about for much longer.'

She gripped the table. 'What do you mean? Is he in some kind of danger?'

Terry tossed some money on to the table. 'Watch my broadcast tonight. You'll find out then.'

The chair crashed to the floor behind her as she leapt to her feet. 'Terry, wait. Is someone out to hurt Midas?'

'It looks like it. Watch the broadcast.'

Then he was gone. She could barely grasp what he'd said. Terry had received a tip-off about a threat to Midas. She wouldn't know any more until she watched his programme tonight. Shaken, she made her way back upstairs.

Georgina was finishing her lunch when Jill came into the kitchen. 'Chicken and pasta. It's yummy,' she declared.

Jill tousled the child's hair. 'I'm glad you like it, sweetheart.' Too keyed up to eat, she refused the housekeeper's offer of lunch for herself. How reliable was Terry's informant? *Was* Midas in danger? She went to the phone.

Her first call was to Midas. Sarah Brent answered, the secretary sounding put out at having to admit that she didn't know where Midas was. 'Two men came and he left a meeting to go with them, just like that,' she said.

Despair gripped Jill. Why did Midas have to be elusive now, of all times? She gave Sarah a message asking Midas to contact her urgently, then hung up.

Bill Downey wasn't much help, either. 'There's nothing about it on the wire service,' he told her. 'But stick with it. It sounds like a hell of a story if there's any truth in it.'

How could she do anything *but* stick with it, when the man she loved was involved? Keeping her panic in check, she thanked Bill and hung up. Perhaps the whole thing was a hoax, dreamed up by Terry to unsettle her. Surely if there was a genuine threat to Midas, word of it would have leaked out by now? The wire services were silent. Perhaps the police knew something.

The officer who answered her call was unhelpful, sounding wary. He didn't deny that there was a problem, she noticed. Either he didn't like journalists or he knew something he wasn't telling. She was becoming paranoid, she told herself when he rang off. The police didn't normally keep secrets from the Press. They might impose an embargo on publication, but they shared information whenever possible. Many of their leads came from the media so it behoved them to co-operate with each other.

That left the possibility of a hoax. Could Terry be so cruel? He could, she conceded, especially where she was concerned.

There was nothing else to do except wait for Terry's evening broadcast. If there was no mention of Midas, then the story was Terry's way of getting even with her.

She passed some of the time playing with Georgina, then they watched *Play School* together on television. Usually such moments were more precious than jewels to Jill, but today she could hardly concentrate. It was a relief to give Georgina her medicine and settle her into bed for a nap. At last, Jill was alone with her tortured thoughts.

The more she tried to focus them, the more they whirled around. Planning for herself and Georgina became impossible. Yet she couldn't stay here much longer. They wouldn't be welcome after Midas saw the article. Where would they go so that Terry wouldn't find them?

Her head jerked up as a key grated in the front door lock. Midas? Her knees went weak as he came in, his face stormy and set. 'Thank goodness, you got my message,' she said, relief flooding her voice.

'What message?'

'You haven't been back to your office? I told Sarah. . .' She faltered as she saw his gaze travel to the newspaper lying open on the coffee-table. So that was why he was here. 'You saw it?'

'Yes, I saw it, although you were a bit late if that's what you wanted to warn me about.'

His words cut through her like a knife. 'It wasn't my doing, I swear.'

His disdainful look raked her. 'You're forgetting that I saw your first draft.'

'It was based on my article, but Terry wrote it over my byline.'

He made a slashing gesture with his hands. 'What does it matter? I haven't time to discuss it now.' He moved towards the stairs.

'Wait. My message wasn't about the story. When Terry came to gloat about it, he mentioned something else, a threat to you.'

A curious light came into his eyes until the lids came down, hooding them. 'What does Casey know about this?'

Horror sent an icy wind shrieking through her soul. 'Then it's true, you *are* in some kind of danger?'

She was about to press for more information when a door swung open and Georgina ambled into the room clutching the teddy bear which she'd taken to bed with her.

The child rubbed her eyes sleepily. 'You woke me up, Mummy. I thought I heard Daddy talking.'

Jill cuddled the sleepy child, pushing the soft blonde curls out of her eyes. 'It wasn't Daddy you heard, darling. It was my friend, who's letting us stay here.'

Georgina peered at him. 'Hello.'

'Hello, Georgina.' His words were warm but he was regarding them both with icy disdain. What on earth was the matter?

'Midas, why are you looking like that?'

'So this was your price.'

The reason for his look became blindingly clear. He thought she had given Terry her notes for the article in exchange for getting Georgina back. Her head swung violently from side to side. 'No, it isn't what you're thinking.'

He ignored her. 'Is "Daddy" due here anytime? Perhaps I cramped your style by turning up early.'

'Of course you didn't. I told you I don't want him to find me.'

'But he managed it somehow. Now you can have your cake and eat it, too.'

'Can I have some cake, too?' The childish interruption silenced her abruptly. How could she argue with him when Georgina was listening to every word?

The front door barrelled open again and the entrance was filled by a tall, solidly built man with a steely-grey crew-cut. Alarm raced through Jill but Midas was unperturbed by the man's arrival. 'I told you I'd be down in a few minutes, Mike, as soon as I collect some things.'

The man frowned. 'A few minutes is up, Mr Thorne. We should be on our way.'

On their way where? Midas still hadn't told her why he was in danger, or who was threatening him. What was going on? She clutched his arm. 'Wait, you can't leave like this.'

The man, Mike, loomed over her. 'We have to, miss. We've already been here too long as it is.'

Surely a business appointment could wait a few more minutes when Midas's safety was at stake? 'Can't you stay long enough to tell me what this is about?' she asked, tears trembling in her voice.

Midas shook his head. 'I have to go. And you should, too. Take your daughter and leave here right away.'

'Can't I stay at least until you get back?'

He gripped her shoulders, hurting her. 'For God's sake, no. Get out of here, do you hear me? I haven't time to argue. Just go.'

So it was over. He didn't want to see her again or hear her side of the story. Blinded by tears, she nodded. 'Very well, Midas. If it's what you want.'

He seemed about to say more but the other man tapped him on the shoulder. 'Come on, for crying out loud.'

With a harsh outpouring of breath, Midas released her and swung around. 'Let's go.'

The door slammed shut behind them, the sound reverberating like a gunshot in the quiet room. She found herself wondering about the other man. He must be important from the way Midas co-operated with him. Perhaps he was involved in the diamond deal.

What did it matter now anyway? Midas had ordered her out of his life, not even allowing her to tell him about Terry's broadcast which might contain vital clues.

'Mummy, what's the matter? Why are you crying?'

The tears had fallen unnoticed until Georgina came up and patted her hand. Jill dashed at the droplets, forcing a smile. 'I'm not crying, darling. There's something in my eye.'

'Why did your friend tell us to go home?'

How could she explain that Midas loathed the sight of her, blaming her for something she hadn't done? She shook her head. 'I don't know, Georgie. Maybe he thought we'd be happier there. What do you think?'

Georgina shook her head. 'I like it right here. I'm going to play with the Barbie dolls some more.'

What was the harm in staying a few more minutes? From the tone of Midas's friend, Mike, their business was pressing so they were unlikely to return for some time. She decided to let Georgina play with the Barbie dolls for a little while. She could use the time to pack their belongings and repair her ravaged make-up.

Tears certainly ruined your looks, she thought, grimacing at her reflection in the bedroom mirror. She looked ninety years old and felt a hundred.

She was smoothing coral lipstick over her mouth, trying not to remember the feel of Midas's lips on hers, when there was a cry from the living-room. 'Look, Mummy, it's Daddy.'

Searing pain tore through her. Was Terry going to make good his promise to take Georgina by force? Then she heard his voice filtered through the television speakers. Georgina must have turned on the television set and caught the trailer for his current affairs programme. His words echoed in her brain. 'Watch the broadcast.' Her heart was in her mouth as she hurried into the living-room.

Georgina watched the screen, her expression rapt. 'Look, it's Daddy.'

'I know, darling. Hush a minute.'

All her attention was riveted on the small screen. '. . .and tonight's main story concerns a series of death threats which have been made against this man.' A head shot of Midas filled the screen. 'Multimillionaire businessman, Michael "Midas" Thorne, is tonight under police guard at an undisclosed location as police investigate the threats which they are taking seriously. For the full story, join me tonight on *Casey's World* at eight-thirty.'

The room whirled around Jill. Someone intended to hurt Midas. She had to find him, to warn him. Then common sense took over. He was already under police protection. The burly man who hustled him away must have been some kind of bodyguard. He would be all right, he had to be. She loved him too much to let it end any other way.

Sharp pains sliced through her palms and she relaxed her fingernails which were digging into her hands. She felt so helpless; wanting desperately to be with him, to share this ordeal with him. The police were doing all they could but what if it wasn't enough?

Georgina packed the Barbie doll and clothes back into their box. 'I'm finished, Mummy. We can go home now.'

Dropping to the carpet, she enfolded the little girl in her arms. 'How would you like to stay here a bit longer?'

The child's eyes shone. 'You mean sleep here? Won't your friend mind?'

'I don't think so, in the circumstances.'

Georgina's features screwed up in concentration. 'What's a circus stance?'

'It means the way things are,' she said. 'And the way things are now, it's better if we stay here.'

'Goody. I like it here.'

Which made two of them, Jill thought unhappily. Midas might be furious when he found her still here, but she couldn't go back to Balmain while he remained under threat. She had to be here in case. . .there was no in case. Nothing was going to happen to him. She was simply going to be here.

She refused to let the housekeeper stay and make dinner for them, insisting she would rather do it herself. It would help to occupy her while she waited for news.

After the staff left for the evening, she heated up a quiche for them both, taking it into the living-room to eat in front of the television set. This way, she could supervise the meal while watching for any developments.

The trailer for Terry's show appeared again with no more facts than before, only adding to her tension. The evening news also reported the threats but said that the police had no leads as to who was responsible. Every time they showed a photograph of Midas her heart missed a beat, until she felt sick with anxiety. Her imagination conjured up faceless men stalking him, bringing him down, his handsome features streaked with blood. She had never been so afraid in her life. If any harm came to him, part of her would die with him.

To keep herself busy, she picked up the scattered toys and bathed Georgina ready for bed, putting her to sleep in the bed she herself had slept in previously. Her daughter insisted on a bedtime story so she dragged out of her memory, the story of the little girl and the angry boys. Georgina identified with the heroine, she noticed, and she hoped the lesson wouldn't be lost on her.

Finally, Georgina snuggled down under the quilt and smiled sleepily as Jill bent over to kiss her. 'Sleep well,' she whispered.

The child's eyelids sagged. 'G'night, Mummy.'

Tiptoeing to the door, Jill dimmed the light and closed the door softly. At least one of them would get some rest tonight. For herself, Jill knew she wouldn't sleep a wink.

She was on her way back to the living-room to resume her vigil by the television set when there was a knock on the front door.

CHAPTER TEN

NERVES jumped in Jill's throat. Could it be over already? 'Is that you, Midas?' she asked through the closed door. But why would he need to knock? He would use his key.

'It is Daniel Prasad,' came the familiar voice.

Relieved, she fumbled the door open. Maybe there was a message for her from Midas. 'Come in, Daniel, I'm so glad to see you.'

He followed her into the living-room and accepted her offer of an orange juice, declining anything alcoholic to drink. 'Have you heard the news?' she asked him.

He drank the juice then set the glass down. 'I heard. How is Mr Thorne bearing up? I take it he is not here?' His dark-eyed glance swept the room then came back to rest on her.

'He's in protective custody until the police find out who's behind the threats,' she explained. 'Who do you think it could be? One of his business partners?'

'It is more likely to be someone he has hurt with his business dealings,' Daniel said flatly.

Her reaction was automatic. 'Midas would never hurt anyone. You should know that.'

'I'm afraid I do not know it, Mrs Casey.'

Her hand flew to her throat. 'How can you say that? Midas is one of the kindest, most generous. . .'

Daniel made a slashing movement with his hand.

'Enough! I see he has hoodwinked you along with the rest of the world.'

Something odd in his voice made her regard him fearfully. 'What are you saying, Daniel?'

'I'm saying he is not the benefactor he likes to appear. He is in league with some terrible people.'

Her head swayed from side to side. 'It's not true. Whose side are you on, anyway?'

'I am on my own side. And unfortunately, it is not the same one as Midas Thorne.'

Terror flowed through her and her bones turned liquid as the implication became clear. 'It's you! You're behind the death threats, aren't you?'

'Very clever, Mrs Casey. Yes, I would like to see him dead. It is only just.'

She sagged on to the couch as her legs buckled under her. 'What harm has Midas ever done to you? He gave you a home, a job.'

'Crumbs from a rich man's table,' he snapped, his eyes flashing. 'Do you think I have always been a menial servant? In Fiji, before the coup, I ran my own helicopter chartering business. My family owned half of Nadi.'

Confusion clouded her vision. 'What has this to do with Midas?'

'Originally, nothing. He wasn't to blame for the coup which left several members of our family dead and all but wiped out our business. I was forced to flee with what I could carry, or I would be in jail at this minute.'

'Were you a criminal?' she asked.

His harsh laugh punctuated the silence. 'One did

not need to commit a crime during the upheavals. One had only to be born the wrong colour.'

She searched her memory for details of the political upheaval Fiji had endured. Racial tension had been acute between Fijian nationals and those of Indian heritage. Many Fijian Indians had fled to other countries, some of them to Australia, after Fiji had been declared a republic. 'Your family must have suffered terribly,' she observed, remembering the accounts she had read.

Her sympathy surprised him. 'We lost everything. I was lucky to escape with my life.'

'And your family?'

'They cannot get permission to leave and join me here. Midas Thorne was supposed to arrange it but he has done nothing.' His eyes glowed like hot coals. 'Now do you see why I must kill him?'

'He has tried, I know he has,' she said, remembering Midas's concern when he explained the problem to her. 'I'm sure it will be all right if you give him more time.'

Daniel's hands spread wide. 'He has had enough time. He manages to do business with the likes of Robert Waya, yet he cannot help my family.'

'That deal was begun before the coup took place,' she tried again. 'He has to honour his word or no one will trust him in business ever again.'

Daniel's dark head inclined in agreement. 'You are quite right, no one will trust him again. Because he will be unable to make any more deals. I had hoped that destroying his partnership would be enough, but it seems I must do more.'

Shock rippled through her as his words penetrated

her fear. 'You gave Terry the story, didn't you?' It was so clear now. Terry's sudden interest in the helicopter. His friendliness towards Daniel. They were calculated to put the pilot at ease.

How well it had worked. Daniel was the only other person besides the principals and herself who knew the whole story. If enough phone calls had been made from the helicopter and enough secret files had been carried back and forth, Daniel could have pieced the details together. By passing them to Terry, he had been hoping to put an end to the deal, knowing that the partners were publicity shy. But it hadn't worked. So now he meant to kill Midas.

Daniel gave a throaty laugh. 'I see you have worked it out. I did give away Mr Thorne's secrets. I thought it would be enough to blow the deal sky-high.'

It had blown her relationship with Midas sky-high, she thought. But Daniel didn't know or care about that. He wanted revenge, blaming Midas for all his troubles. Her glance flickered to the telephone. If only she could call someone, warn Midas.

Her face must have betrayed her thoughts because Daniel moved between her and the telephone. 'Would you like to telephone your beloved?'

He still thought she was Midas's mistress. She was torn between pride in her love for Midas and the awful realisation that she could be used to destroy him. Common sense won. 'It's not the way you think. He doesn't care for me. He. . .he told me to be gone from here before he returned.'

Blotches of darker colour appeared on Daniel's cheeks. 'You must think me stupid, Mrs Casey. I know you two are lovers. Is it not so?'

Did it show so clearly? It was useless to protest further so she inclined her head. 'Yes. I love him. But he doesn't love me. You must believe me.'

He gave a sinister smile. 'We will soon put it to the test, isn't it so?'

'What are you going to do?'

She was afraid that she already knew what he had in mind and his next words confirmed her suspicions. 'You must bring Midas Thorne to me. I think he will come back if he knows your life is in danger, yes?'

Her throat was painfully dry but she made herself frame the question. 'Is my life in danger?'

'I'm afraid it is.'

Reaching inside his jacket, he withdrew a wicked-looking hand-gun. The dull grey metal glinted in the electric light and panic clawed at her stomach. 'Are you going to shoot me?'

'Not as long as you play your part.'

Unable to tear her gaze away from the gun, she could only nod. Then despair gripped her as a piping voice came from the other room. 'Mummy! I want a drink of water.'

Daniel's smile widened. 'It is even better than I thought. Is the child a relative of Mr Thorne's?'

'No, she's my daughter,' she said through parched lips.

He nodded as if pleased by her answer. 'Give her the drink. But be quick and do not do anything clever if you wish her to remain safe. Then I wish you to make a telephone call.'

She took as long as she dared to fetch the glass of water for Georgina, who immediately settled back down to sleep, to Jill's huge relief. When she could delay no longer, she returned to the living-room. Daniel instructed her to call the police and demand that Midas be brought to the apartment.

'Has he threatened you or the child?' the calm voice queried once she made Daniel's demands known.

'He has a gun,' she stated and heard the indrawn gasp at the other end. 'What should I do now?'

'Just do whatever he tells you to until we get there. And don't. . .' There was a scuffle at the other end then the policeman surrendered the phone to someone else.

'Jill, are you all right?'

Weakness invaded her limbs and she sagged against the telephone table. 'Oh, God, it's good to hear your voice.' She was careful not to use Midas's name but Daniel was alerted by the change in her tone. 'I'm so frightened.'

'I thought I told you to get out of there.'

'I know, but I couldn't leave, not like this.' Even now, all he cared about was sending her away. Panic rose inside her like a cloud. 'You mustn't come here. Whatever they say, don't let them bring you here. Please. . .'

The phone was wrenched from her grasp and she was pushed heavily on to the couch. Daniel spoke into the phone. 'I know you are there, Thorne. For the sake of the woman and child, I hope you will listen to me and not her. You have thirty minutes to get here.' He slammed the receiver down.

'How do you know it's long enough for him to get here?' she asked, her voice trembling with the effort of maintaining control.

'I don't. It is up to them to find a way.' His clipped, metallic tones terrified her. He sounded like a robot, intent on his mission. He really intended to kill Midas. It would be all over as soon as he walked through the front door.

Hysterical laughter bubbled in her throat. Daniel thought Midas's love for her would lure him here. How wrong he was! Midas hated her. In the midst of this nightmare, he could still order her out of his life.

She was sorry now that she hadn't left when he told her to. Without her, Daniel would have no hostages to use against Midas. By staying, she had placed him in terrible danger. Her own life hardly seemed to matter. If it hadn't been for Georgina, she might have attempted to escape. Anything would be better than sitting here, waiting for the man she loved to walk into a trap with her as the bait.

The minutes ticked past. 'This isn't the way, Daniel,' she tried.

'This is the only way,' he said. He played with the safety-catch on his gun, clicking it on and off with terrifying precision. The cold, inhuman sound chilled her blood.

Mesmerised, she stared at the gun. 'Please, could you stop doing that? I'm already scared out of my wits.'

'Very well.' To her astonishment, he flicked the safety catch back on and this time left it in place. He had some human feelings, after all.

An impulse took hold of her. 'Tell me about your family. How many children did you say you have?'

His mask-like expression eased fractionally. 'I have

four children. Three boys and a girl. The boys are ten, nine and seven. The girl six.'

'The same age as my daughter,' she said. 'And your wife? What's her name?'

He regarded her warily. 'I do not wish to talk about them. You are wasting your time.'

'Don't you understand? If you do what you're planning to do——' She couldn't bring herself to say it out loud. 'You may never see them again. You'll be locked up in an Australian gaol. They won't even be able to visit you, perhaps for years.'

He shrugged. 'What happens to me is of no consequence. My children will know that I sacrificed myself for them.'

It sounded as if he didn't care whether he lived or died. Her eyes closed on a wave of despair. How could she reason with such a fanatic? Her arms locked around her body and she began to rock back and forth, holding in a tidal wave of tears. If she gave in to it now, she would never stop crying.

'Stop that noise,' Daniel said sharply, standing up. Had he heard something? Her heart almost stopped at the thought that it could be Midas.

Daniel strode to the door, the pistol hugged to his chest. For the first time, she noticed the bulky shape of a silencer at the end of the barrel.

Flattening himself against one side of the door, he called out, 'Who is it? Who's there?'

'Midas Thorne.'

Oh, God, no! She wasn't aware of leaping to her feet until Daniel motioned her to sit down. She perched on the edge of the couch, her heart hammering painfully against her ribs. She couldn't just sit here while Midas was gunned down in cold blood. She had to do something. But what?

A key scratched in the lock and Daniel brought the gun up until it was level with the centre of the door.

Slowly, like an image in a dream, the door swung open and a tall, barrel-chested man stood there. She glimpsed the flashing cobalt eyes and glossy dark hair brushed to one side. The midnight-blue suit and pin-striped shirt were achingly familiar, as was the red club tie he'd been wearing when he left this afternoon.

She absorbed it all in the split-second before Daniel's finger tightened on the trigger. Then she knew what she had to do. With a scream of anguish, she threw herself across the room, putting her body between the gunman and Midas.

'No, don't,' she screamed, pushing Midas as hard as she could back into the corridor. She was no match for his muscular build but her momentum carried him backwards. The shot which Daniel loosed off went wild, burying itself in the wallpaper of the hallway above Midas's head.

Powerful arms caught her and pulled her out of the line of fire. There was another thunking sound, as a silenced bullet was fired, then a scuffle and a gun span across the carpet, landing near Jill's feet. Suddenly there were men everywhere. One of them scooped up the weapon, holding it gingerly by a handkerchief looped through the trigger. Another man marched Daniel out of the apartment, his hands pulled up high behind his back. The strong arms were still around her and she collapsed against the man's chest. 'Is it over?'

The man holding Daniel gave a grim nod. 'It's over, thanks to you, Mrs Casey.'

Thanks to her? In a rush she realised she had saved the man she loved. She drank in the sight of her beloved, safe and whole, his back turned to her as he spoke to someone inside the apartment. She struggled against the arms which restrained her. 'Let me go, I have to go to him.'

Inexplicably, the hold on her tightened. 'I may have something to say about that.'

Bewildered, she looked up. The man holding her was dressed in an unfamiliar sweater and jeans, yet the face which looked down at her so fondly belonged to Midas. Her glance went to the man in the mid-night-blue suit. 'But I thought. . .'

'You thought it was me, I know. He's from the tactical response group, in my borrowed clothes with a bullet-proof vest underneath. As soon as I knew you were inside with that madman, I wanted to break the door down with my bare hands. But the experts insisted on doing it their way.' His hands stroked the hair away from her forehead. 'They reckoned without you, though.'

Her muscles weakened as she realised it was Midas himself holding her so tightly. The man wearing his clothes was a police decoy. She clung to Midas, hardly daring to believe that the crisis was over.

A member of the tactical response group came up to them. 'Is she OK? Shall I get the doctor up here?'

'I'm fine,' she said shakily. 'I don't need a doctor.' All she needed was the assurance of Midas's arms around her. He was safe. Nothing else mattered. She allowed him to help her back into the apartment and on to the couch. His hold didn't slacken.

Cupping a hand under her chin, he lifted her to face him. 'How's Georgina?'

She gave a shaky laugh. 'She slept through the whole thing. I was terrified in case she woke up and came out.'

He felt the tremors start and pulled her to him, smoothing her hair back with a comforting gesture. 'It's all right, don't think about it. It's over now.'

Yes, it was, she thought bleakly. Now that Daniel had been caught and Midas was safe, he would remember that she wasn't supposed to be here. He was only holding her out of compassion, as one might comfort a victim of any crisis, even when they meant nothing to you. She stirred restively. 'I suppose the police will want a statement from me.'

'Tomorrow will be soon enough for that,' he assured her. 'I'll take you to see them myself.'

Her bleak gaze met his. 'Then you don't mind if I stay here for another night?'

'Good lord, no.' The explosive force of his answer caught her by surprise. 'What makes you think I would mind?'

'You told me to go,' she reminded him. 'I know you didn't want me to stay here, but I couldn't bring myself to leave while you were in danger.'

He groaned in frustration. 'The danger was the very reason I didn't want you here. Without knowing who was behind the plot, the police advised against telling anyone what was going on, so I could only warn you to get away. If you'd left when I told you to, this wouldn't have happened.'

'You didn't really think I was in on it, did you?'

'I told the police it wasn't you, and then you proved it by saving my life.'

'Not you, a decoy.'

'You didn't know that. When I think of you putting yourself between me and a bullet, my blood runs cold. Could you really care about me as much as that?'

More than he could imagine. 'I love you,' she said simply, no longer caring whether he welcomed the news or not. 'I found it out when we made love on your boat. I know it can't lead to anything, but I can't change the way I feel.'

There, it was out in the open. He was staring at her in open-mouthed astonishment, oblivious of the police team working around them. 'Why should I want to change how you feel?'

'Our relationship was supposed to be a sham. By the time I realised it wasn't, it was too late. I'd fallen in love with you.'

'Why didn't you say something?'

'I didn't think you wanted to hear it. The article seemed to be the last straw. When you told me to go, I was sure you hated me.'

'Never that, my love. Never that. I think I've loved you from the moment we met on the stairwell.'

Surprise clouded her gaze and she blinked hard. 'You love me? But. . . I'm a journalist. The enemy, remember?'

The harsh planes and angles of his face became more forbidding than she had ever seen them. His tormented gaze locked with hers and she wondered if she had destroyed their fragile rapport with her reminder. But he shook his head. 'No, you're not the enemy. I've been deluding myself for far too long.'

What was he trying to say? She straightened and studied him in bewilderment. 'I don't understand. You had a perfect right to hate my profession, after what happened to your wife and child.'

Before he could frame an answer, the leader of the tactical response group interrupted them. 'I hate to disturb the happy reunion, but we're finished here, Mr Thorne.'

Midas slid her on to the seat beside him, keeping his arm around her shoulders as he held his free hand out to the man. 'Thanks for everything, Mike.'

Mike? She recognised the burly man who'd accompanied Midas to the apartment earlier. The man grinned. 'I wish they all ended as happily as this one. Makes my job a lot easier.'

'What will happen to Daniel?' she asked Mike.

'He'll be charged, of course. But if he's found guilty maybe he'll be sent back to Fiji, rather than serving time here.'

She found herself hoping that he would. His method had been wrong, but, more than anyone, she understood how driven he must have been. At least if he was sent back to Fiji he would be close to his family.

She remained on the couch while Midas farewelled the police team. The apartment was a mess after the invasion, but nothing mattered as much as being with Midas. He had called her his love. Had it been the heat of the moment or did he really mean it? She had saved his life. He could have been speaking out of some crazy sense of indebtedness. She gnawed the tips of her fingers in frustration.

But no sooner had Midas closed the door on the police team, than there was a bewildered cry from the door of the bedroom. 'Mummy, I thought I heard some noises.'

She swept the little girl into her arms, shooting Midas a warning glance. 'It's nothing, darling. Just the television set. You can go back to bed now. Come on, I'll tuck you in.'

Without protest, the sleepy child accepted the explanation and let herself be led back to bed, where she was soon tucked in again. Thinking of the danger they'd been in tonight, Jill had to fight the urge to clutch the little girl to her. She settled for stroking the small forehead as Georgina's long lashes drooped over fast-closing eyes. 'Sleep now,' she murmured. 'I'll be in the next room if you need me.'

She smoothed the covers over the small body and dropped a kiss on her forehead, then started to back out of the room. Midas came up behind her and his arms encircled her, as he looked over her shoulder to the sleeping child. 'She'll never know what she missed,' he said softly.

Her hands clutched his. 'I hope not.'

Quietly they withdrew to the living-room, pulling the connecting door shut. 'What I don't understand is what she's doing here,' Midas said when they sat down again.

Hugging her arms around herself, she explained about finding Jennifer and Terry together, smoking pot. 'I couldn't leave her with that,' she said, then shuddered. 'When I think of the worse danger I placed her in. . .'

Midas moved closer, his arms closing around her. 'Sshh. You didn't know. If anything, Casey is the one to blame, not you.'

Her questioning glance sought his. 'Terry—why?'

'He knew about the threat to me before anyone else did. He could have warned you about Daniel so you could get Georgina safely away.'

Some of the tension drained out of her. 'He could, couldn't he? Or at least he could have gone to the police with what he knew, instead of letting it come to this. But he didn't. The story was more important to him that our safety.'

'It was Daniel who gave him the information about the diamond coating process, wasn't it,' Midas stated rather than asked.

Her long lashes fluttered upwards. 'You guessed it wasn't me?'

'When I had time to think about it, I was sure you'd never do anything so underhand. So that left your ex-husband. I've been worried about Daniel for some time, knowing how he felt about his family. But I had no idea he was this close to a complete breakdown.'

'Terry must have discovered Daniel's state of mind, yet he did nothing about it,' she concurred.

Midas looked grim. 'Except that Casey wasn't as smart as he thought. Instead of manipulating the pilot, Terry himself was the one being manipulated. Daniel was using him as a mouthpiece all along.'

Jill nodded. 'Terry would hate to admit it, but you're probably right.'

He laughed drily. 'Perhaps in return for keeping the details quiet, he would consider giving you custody of your daughter.'

Her eyes shone. 'Maybe he would.' Terry was vain enough to want his part in this kept quiet. And now he knew how a child cramped his style with the Jennifers in his life, maybe fatherhood had lost some of its appeal. Flutterings of hope stirred inside her. If anyone could persuade Terry, it was Midas. She snuggled close against him.

'I think I'd enjoy having a ready-made family,' Midas observed. 'Do you think Georgina will accept me as a guardian?'

'She's her mother's daughter,' Jill said shyly. 'We tend to like the same things.'

'Like or love?' His voice deepened, sending shivers down her spine.

'Definitely love,' she affirmed. 'Oh, Midas, I do love you.'

'Then you will marry me?'

Her head lifted and she regarded him apprehensively. Love was one thing, but marriage was a giant step. 'Are you sure?' she asked.

His sigh whispered between them. 'Don't tell me you still have doubts? I couldn't stand to lose you now.'

'I have no doubts about the way I feel. But I thought you did.' She lowered her eyes and toyed with the buckle on his belt, forcing herself to add, 'I'm still a journalist, Midas. I could give it up—but are you sure it won't come between us?'

'Never. That's what I wanted to tell you when

Mike interrupted. I've been blaming the wrong people for Yolande's death.'

'I don't understand.'

He searched inside himself for the right words. 'I was as much at fault as anyone. When I married Yolande, I knew she was a simple country girl. Life was fine as long as we lived in the mining towns. When my business took off, she didn't want to move to the city but she did, for my sake. Because she didn't complain, I assumed that she had adjusted.'

Jill's mind flashed back to the photos of Yolande. Her instinct had been the correct one. Yolande hadn't been able to cope with Midas's success. 'What about your child?' she asked.

'I didn't know it at the time, but Yolande only had the baby to please me. Her earlier attempts to become pregnant had ended in miscarriages but she kept trying for my sake, even though I told her I was happy with our life the way it was. Right up until Michael Junior was born, she was so happy that I thought she'd made the right choice. Then she plunged into a terrifying depression. Nothing seemed to reach her. If I'd talked her out of having a child, she might be alive today.'

Jill's hand sought his and her fingers tightened around him. 'Even if you had, it wouldn't necessarily have made any difference.'

'I'll never know, will I?' His voice was harsh with bitterness. She ached to comfort him and banish the pain she could see in his eyes as he looked down at her. 'So you see, I can't entirely blame the journalists who followed us to Byron Bay. They were only doing their job. I should have been more alert to the mental state she was in. Tonight, worrying about you, I finally faced the truth.'

'It's over now,' she said gently. 'Can't you forgive yourself and go on?'

'It's a hell of a burden, but now I have a reason to try.'

Chaos screamed through her brain. She could barely absorb the full import of his admission. He didn't blame her, or any of her profession, for his loss. The last barrier between them crumbled into nothing. Happiness swelled inside her like a living thing. 'Oh, Midas, I love you so much. It breaks my heart to see you blaming yourself for a tragedy which no one could have foreseen. Yolande did what she wanted, no matter what the outcome. She wanted to make you happy and I'm sure that's what she'd want for you now.'

'Then say you'll marry me,' he insisted. 'Nothing could make me happier than that.'

Her last doubts melted away. As long as they loved each other, they had all they needed to embark on a lifetime of happiness together. 'Yes, yes and yes,' she repeated. Her hand still rested on his belt buckle and she became aware of a stirring in him which started the blood racing in her veins.

His mouth sought hers with hungry abandon and they clung together. She was on fire with her love for him and her parted lips told him so. His breath was the kiss of life, filling her with new vitality. She linked her hands behind the thick column of his neck, tasting his warm breath like wine more heady than any drink she'd ever tasted. His leg lay heavily across her body but it was a blessed burden, reminding her that she belonged to him now and for all time.

When the sweet torment became too much to bear, he claimed her, gently at first, building to a driving passion which swept her along on a torrent of mind-tearing sensations. He loved her. The refrain beat at her mind, over and over, in time with his passion, until she was filled with the wondrous certainty that nothing could come between them ever again.

Much later, as they lay in each other's arms, a crack of light spilled across their entwined bodies, and a small voice called, 'I want a drink of water.' Laughter rippled between them. Well, maybe just one thing. . .

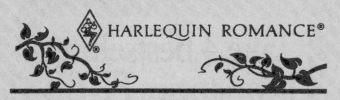

HARLEQUIN ROMANCE®

After her father's heart attack, Stephanie Bloomfield comes
home to Orchard Valley, Oregon, to be with him and with
her sisters.

Orchard Valley

Steffie learns that many things have changed in her
absence—but not her feelings for journalist Charles
Tomaselli. He was the reason she left Orchard Valley. Now,
three years later, will he give her a reason to stay?

"The Orchard Valley trilogy features three delightful, spirited
sisters and a trio of equally fascinating men. The stories are rich
with the romance, warmth of heart and humor readers expect,
and invariably receive, from Debbie Macomber."
—Linda Lael Miller

Don't miss the Orchard Valley trilogy by Debbie Macomber:

VALERIE   Harlequin Romance #3232 (November 1992)
STEPHANIE   Harlequin Romance #3239 (December 1992)
NORAH   Harlequin Romance #3244 (January 1993)

Look for the special cover flash on each book!

Available wherever Harlequin books are sold.   ORC-2

HARLEQUIN PRESENTS®

A Year Down Under

Beginning in January 1993, some of Harlequin Presents's most exciting authors will join us as we celebrate the land down under by featuring one title per month set in Australia or New Zealand.

Intense, passionate romances, these stories will take you from the heart of the Australian outback to the wilds of New Zealand, from the sprawling cattle and sheep stations to the sophistication of cities like Sydney and Auckland.

Share the adventure—and the romance— of A Year Down Under!

Don't miss our first visit in HEART OF THE OUTBACK by Emma Darcy, Harlequin Presents #1519, available in January wherever Harlequin Books are sold.   YDU-G

HARLEQUIN HISTORICAL
CHRISTMAS
·STORIES·1992·

Capture the magic and romance of Christmas in the 1800s with HARLEQUIN HISTORICAL CHRISTMAS STORIES 1992, a collection of three stories by celebrated historical authors. The perfect Christmas gift!

Don't miss these heartwarming stories, available in November wherever Harlequin books are sold:

MISS MONTRACHET REQUESTS by Maura Seger
CHRISTMAS BOUNTY by Erin Yorke
A PROMISE KEPT by Bronwyn Williams

Plus, as an added bonus, you can receive a FREE keepsake Christmas ornament. Just collect four proofs of purchase from any November or December 1992 Harlequin or Silhouette series novels, or from any Harlequin or Silhouette Christmas collection, and receive a beautiful dated brass Christmas candle ornament.

Mail this certificate along with four (4) proof-of-purchase coupons plus $1.50 postage and handling (check or money order—do not send cash), payable to Harlequin Books, to: **In the U.S.**: P.O. Box 9057, Buffalo, NY 14269-9057; **In Canada**: P.O. Box 622, Fort Erie, Ontario, L2A 5X3.

ONE PROOF OF PURCHASE

Name: _____
_____
Address: _____
_____
City: _____
State/Province: _____
Zip/Postal Code: _____

HX92POP   093 KAG